# BREATH *by* BREATH

NEW YORK TIMES BESTSELLING AUTHOR

## KAYLEE RYAN

Cover Design: Lori Jackson Design
Cover Photography: Furious Fotog
Editing: Hot Tree Editing
Proofreading: Deaton Author Services, Jo Thompson, Jess Hodge
Paperback Formatting: Integrity Formatting

# CHAPTER
*Lena*
## ONE

*Seventeen years old. Where it all began.*

**T**ODAY MARKS THE first of a new journey. A new school for my senior year of high school. I hate I had to leave all of my friends behind, but I understand why we had to move.

Six months ago, we lost my father to cancer. One day, he was this vibrant, full-of-life man, and the next, he was lying in a hospital bed as we said our last goodbyes.

I hate cancer.

My mom stuck it out to let me finish the school year, but the house was too big for her to afford on her own. My father had life insurance, but medical bills and the burial took most of it. So, that means my mom and I had to pack up our lives and move to a smaller house. That just so happens to be in a little town just south of Nashville. A little town that's forty minutes from my old high school but closer to my mom's work.

I didn't scream and yell or act out like most kids my age. I understand why we had to do it. I don't like it, but it's what we had to do in order to be able to survive on my mom's salary alone. She's a nurse at a surgery center. She makes good money, or that's what she tells me, just not enough. I understand this is what we needed to do.

I hate this move almost as much as I hate cancer.

Anyway, that brings me to this moment. I'm standing in front of the bathroom mirror, fussing over my hair. It's my senior year, and I have no friends. I don't know a single soul in this new school, and I'm nervous. When Mom asks, I tell her it will be fine, and I know that it will be. Life has a way of working out. What I don't tell her is that my insides have been churning for a week, dreading walking into that school on my own.

"Lena!" Mom yells from the kitchen. "It's time to go. You don't want to be late on your first day."

I sigh and take one last look in the mirror before turning off the light. I rush across the hall to my bedroom and grab my backpack. I do a quick look, making sure I have my house key, everything the school said I would need for today, and money for lunch. I'm supposed to report to the office to get my class schedule, and lists will be provided by the teachers for any other supplies we might need for classes.

"It's only one year," I mutter as I slowly head toward the kitchen where my mom will be waiting in her scrubs, with her brown hair pulled back in a ponytail and her tumbler of piping-hot, way-too-sweet coffee in her hand.

"You look beautiful." Her eyes mist with tears as she smiles, and I give her a watery smile of my own.

Neither of us needs to say it, but we both wish Dad was here. He's supposed to be here for this — to watch me start my final year of high school. I don't let myself go there. I can't think about all the things he's going to miss. That's an emotional journey I can't take today.

Instead, I hike my backpack over my shoulder, grab the bottle of water and protein bar Mom laid out for me on the counter, and smile at my mother. "Ready?"

"You're going to be great, Lena."

"Of course I am." We both know that my confidence is false, but neither one of us mentions it. Fake it until you make it or until the end of your senior year. You know, whichever comes first.

"Are you sure you don't want me to drive you?"

Inwardly, I shudder at the thought. "Mom, I'm fine. You'll be late for work. Besides, I can't be the new girl who's going to be eighteen in a few weeks and lets her mommy drive her to school."

She laughs at that. "Fine, be safe. You have your house key, right?"

"I do. I'll see you when you get home."

"I love you, Lena."

"Love you too, Mom." I don't stick around for more words. We're both ragged with emotions, and we need to get on with our days.

Pulling open the door of my Jeep, I climb behind the wheel. Every time I do, I think of my dad. I can still remember the day he pulled up to the house in this Jeep. He got out and handed me the keys before wrapping his arms around my mother and kissing her temple. I stood there in shock while they smiled at me. He was healthy, then, but that changed not long after.

"Love you, Daddy," I whisper as I start my Jeep and carefully pull out onto the road.

The drive to the school is a short one. Ten minutes later, I'm easing into the parking lot. I don't give myself a single second to let fear and anxiety take over. I quickly grab my things, pull the key from the ignition, and climb out. I lock the doors and make my way inside.

The hallways are bustling with students, all excitedly talking about their summers. I keep my head held high and follow the signs to the main office. I push open the door. The room is much quieter, muffling the sounds of the hallway I just left behind. I stand in the small line, waiting my turn. When I step up to the counter, I smile at the receptionist.

"Hi, my name is Lena Hartford. This is my first day. I was told to stop here to get my schedule."

"Hi, Lena, welcome." She types on her computer and smiles with a slight nod as the printer whirs to life, and she reaches behind her to grab what I assume is my schedule. "Here you go, dear. If you have any issues at all, you come right back to see me. Now, let me see who your buddy is going to be."

"My buddy?"

"Yeah, we pull another senior from first period study hall and have them give you a tour of the school. We've found it much easier if a peer does the tour instead of the office staff. Makes newcomers like yourself feel more at ease and helps you meet new people." She offers me a kind smile, which I return. I'm not sure if her theory is correct, but meeting new people and not feeling like an outcast is super appealing.

I'm standing off to the side, staring out the window, waiting for whoever it is that's going to take me under their wing this morning. I hope whoever it is, he or she is nice and aren't all angry and broody that they're missing their study hall catch-up time with their friends to show me around. The last thing I need is to make an enemy on day one.

"Mrs. G, you're looking as beautiful as ever," a masculine voice says behind me.

I don't turn to look. Whoever he is, he's probably trying to charm his way into something.

"Mr. Riggins, what can I do for you this morning?"

"I'm here for you, Mrs. G. Mr. Harper sent me from study hall." Great, Mr. Smooth is my tour guide. I still don't turn to look. Instead, I choose to keep my eyes trained out the window.

"Oh, well, I thought Abigail was on the rotation list for this week."

"She is, but she has a headache, so I volunteered."

"All right, but, Stanley Riggins, I'm warning you now. You must be on your best behavior. Don't make me call your momma."

"Mrs. G.," he gasps as if he's offended. It's hilarious, and I have to bite down on my lip to keep a chuckle from escaping. This guy, he's full of confidence, and just from this conversation alone, I know he's trouble.

"Fair enough. Lena Hartford, this is Stanley Riggins. He's going to show you around the school and help you identify each of your classrooms."

Time's up.

I turn my gaze to the kind receptionist. "Thank you, Mrs. Garrison." I give her a kind smile before turning to look at Mr. Suave. I open my mouth to say hello, but I can't seem to find my voice. Standing before me is the hottest guy I've ever seen. He's tall, well over six feet, with dark hair and broad shoulders.

"Lena." He says my name like a caress. His eyes are locked with mine, and suddenly, it's hard to breathe.

I swallow thickly. "Yes. That's me. Lena." I point to my chest, and my face flames with embarrassment. I clear my throat. "It's nice to meet you." I offer him my hand, remembering my manners, and he doesn't hesitate to take it.

Instantly, there's a spark that ignites between us. His eyes flare, and he whispers, "Magic." His eyes are wide, and his grip on my hand is firm.

I don't hate it.

"Go on now. You've got all of first period to show her around. I expect you both in your second-period classes." Mrs. G shoos us out of the room.

I'm shocked when Stanley laces his fingers through mine, an intimate gesture as he leads me out of the office into the now-quiet hallway. He guides me to the end of the hall, away from any windows, and stops. He stands still, his eyes raking over me. He stops at our joined hands.

"Where you from, Lena?" he asks softly. He lifts his gaze from our hands, waiting patiently for my answer.

My throat is dry, but I manage to answer, "Tennessee. About forty minutes from here."

He nods. "You here for good?"

I return his nod. "Yeah." I don't get into why I'm here, and right now, Stanley doesn't seem to care about that either.

"You got a boyfriend waiting for you forty minutes from here?" He takes a step closer, putting us toe-to-toe as he tilts his head to the side. Again, he waits as if we have all the time in the world for my reply.

"N-No."

A slow, sexy grin pulls at his lips. "Good. That means I don't have any competition." He winks, and a million butterflies take flight in my belly. I've never responded this way to anyone before.

Why Stanley? Why this guy? Why now? When my world has been uprooted, and I'm trying to find my footing.

"What?" I ask, not sure I heard him right. I let myself get lost in my thoughts. Surely, he didn't say what I thought he did.

"You and me, we're going to do great things." His voice is husky, and his gaze is intense, as if the words he speaks are some unwritten rule.

"I'm not having sex with you," I blurt. I'm embarrassed, but he might as well know his efforts are wasted. I'm not that kind of girl, no matter how hot he is or how many butterflies he causes to flutter inside me.

He smiles at my outburst. "Do you believe in magic, Lena?"

I have whiplash from this guy. "When I was a kid, maybe." I shrug. How did we go from talking about sex to magic? My head is spinning as I try to decipher this moment with him.

"Yeah," he agrees. "I didn't used to believe in it either."

"What changed your mind?" I find myself asking. For some strange reason, I need to understand why he's suddenly spouting about magic and how he suddenly believes. What am I missing?

He lifts his hand, which isn't holding mine, and presses it against my cheek. His eyes bore into mine. "You."

# CHAPTER

*Stanley*

# TWO

I DON'T THINK I've ever felt skin this soft. My Lena, my magic, stands still as I rest my hand against her cheek. All these years, I swore my dad was just talking shit, but he was right. It happened in an instant. Gramps says it took longer for him, but for me, as soon as she turned around, I could feel it in my soul.

Feel her.

If my buddies could hear me now, they'd give me shit, of that I'm certain. They're all about sleeping around and playing the field. I'm not into playing games with someone's heart, and definitely not with hers.

"Me?" she whispers. Her eyes are wide, and I can see the confusion in their blue depths.

All I can do is smile at her. I can't explain it, because, in truth, I don't really understand it myself. All I know is that my dad and my gramps both said I would know when I've found my magic. That's this moment, standing here with the beautiful Lena.

*She's my magic.*

"Come on. I'll show you around." I drop my hand from her cheek, instantly missing the feel of her soft skin. "Can I see your schedule?"

Her hands have a slight tremble when she hands it to me. I want to tell her that I'm not crazy. I know what she's thinking. For the last eighteen years, I've thought the same thing. The men in my family were crazy, talking about magic all the time. Each time, my mom and my grams would just smile and nod, accepting their crazy stories of love. I thought they were just indulging them, but now I know better.

Pushing thoughts of my family out of my mind, I focus on my girl's schedule. "You have all but one class with me." I smile up at her. "This way." I keep her hand in mine. PDA warnings from teachers be damned as I lead us down the hall to where I was before I volunteered to take Abigail's place this morning. "This is study hall. We're in there together."

"Okay." Her reply is soft, but the look on her face tells me she's concentrating. She has a determined look about her, and I'm sure she's processing and memorizing where she's supposed to go each day.

"Hey." I give her hand a gentle squeeze. "I'll be here to guide you. Every class, I'll make sure you get to where you need to go."

"You don't have to do that."

I wonder if her lips are as soft as they look. "I want to. Come on, let's go through the rest of your schedule."

"The only class we don't have together is the last one. You're in Home Economics, and I'm in shop class. I'll walk you, and they're in the same hall, so I'll be waiting for you when class is over. Did you drive?"

"I drove."

"Good. We won't have to rush to get you to your bus."

"You really don't have to walk me to all of my classes," she says. "I appreciate you showing me around. I should be okay." She seems flustered and a little confused at my announcement.

"Oh, I'm walking you. Not just today but for the rest of the year. What kind of boyfriend would I be if I didn't?"

"Boyfriend?" Her eyes grow wide, and her mouth hangs open in shock.

"Well, not yet, technically. I need to ask you, and you need to make me work for it. Nothing worth having comes easy. That's what my dad always says. Besides, I need to prove to you that the magic is real. All I ask is that you let me. That you don't entertain seeing anyone else until I've had my chance to do that?" She seems to freeze at my admission. Her gaze is distant before she brings it back to me.

"I don't know that I'm emotionally there. My life has been — hard." Her confession is whispered, and a little haunted.

I want to demand that she tell me everything, but I slow my roll. I'm coming on strong and can hear my dad's voice in my head telling me to give her some breathing room. I don't want to give her room. I want everyone in this damn school to know she's mine.

I take a slow, deep breath and pull her into my arms. Instead of demanding to know what's been hard in her life, I give her the solace of my embrace instead. I let her feel through my touch that I'm going to be her safe place to land. That's what my mom and Grams say about Dad and Gramps, and I plan to be that for Lena.

"You take all the time you need. I'll be right here." Unable to help myself, I place a kiss on the top of her head before releasing her. "Come on." I step back and take her hand in mine. She stands still, staring at our joined hands, as if she can't believe she's let me touch her. "Let me show you the cafeteria. We have the same lunch period, so I can introduce you to my friends then." I start to walk away, but she doesn't move. I stop and turn to look at her, and she pulls her hand from mine, taking a couple of steps back. I know I'm coming on strong, but I can't help it.

"I don't know why you're being so nice to me. This isn't at all what I expected on my first day. The hottest guy in school doesn't usually want anything to do with me. I'm plain Jane. Nothing remarkable about me. So, please, Stanley Riggins, if this is some kind of 'new girl' joke, please, I beg you to walk away." Tears well in her eyes, and my heart squeezes painfully inside my chest. "I've had enough heartbreak for a lifetime." Her voice cracks, and so does my heart.

I turn back around and take the two steps to stand toe-to-toe with her. Placing my index finger beneath her chin, I lift so our gazes connect. Beautiful bright blue orbs full of pain, and if I'm not mistaken, hope, peer back at me.

My heart is racing because I hate the thought of her in pain. Lifting her hand, which isn't securely enclosed in mine, I place it flat on my chest. Her eyes widen a fraction and I know she can feel how fast my heart is beating.

"This is not a joke or a game. I'm not that guy, Lena. I will never be that guy. I want to get to know you. I want you to give me all of your time and attention, and in turn, I'll give you all of me. I want to know that you'll give me a fair shot at being yours."

"You want to be mine?" She says it like it's the craziest thing she's ever heard, and maybe it is, but it doesn't make it less true.

"Only yours." I stare deep into her eyes, willing her to trust me.

She's quiet, studying me. I stand still, holding her hand in mine while pressing the other against my chest, and give her all the time she needs. The bell is going to ring soon, and I'm going to have to take us to our next class. I hope she finds whatever she's looking for before that happens.

"We need to slow this train down a little."

"I'll take this as slow as you want. Just promise me one thing."

"What's that?"

"It's just me. You give me that chance to let you see I mean what I say. Think of us as exclusively seeing where things go." I wink, trying to lighten the mood.

She laughs. "Okay. Just—give me some time."

"Time." I nod. I feel as if a ton of bricks have been lifted off my shoulders. She's mine, or she will be. "I can give you a lifetime." The words are out of my mouth before I can stop them. She shakes her head, amused, but I mean it. I feel the spark that ignites between us. The air is charged. She's it.

She's my magic.

The bell rings, and without another word, I lead her to our next class. I pull us to the back of the room and sit in the chair next to hers. All of my buddies come over to say hi, and I introduce them. I'm aware of the looks I'm getting from my fellow classmates and teachers, but I don't care.

All day, she's right next to me. When I have to drop her off at her last class, I'm tempted to go to the office and ask to switch to home economics. Lena just laughs at my suggestion and pushes me down the hall as she enters the room without me. By the time the bell rings, I'm full of nervous energy. I jump out of my seat, rush two doors down, and wait for her.

"Hey." I'm going for casual, but we both know I had to work to get through the throng of students to be here this fast.

"Stanley."

"Lena."

She grins, and it lights up her face. "I guess you're going to walk me to my car?"

"What kind of boyfriend would I be if I didn't?"

"Not my boyfriend," she tosses back with a lighthearted laugh. She glances over at Gail, the girl she was talking to. She's a sweet girl. We've gone to school together our entire lives. I'm glad she's being nice to my girl. At least she appears to be. "I'll see you tomorrow."

Gail flashes her a wide smile. "Yep, and you can bet we're going to talk about this." She waves her hand between Lena and me.

"Nothing to talk about," Lena tells her.

"Uh-huh. Take care of my new friend, Stanley Riggins."

"Always, Liz."

"Not my boyfriend," Lena says once Gail has walked away. There's humor dancing in her eyes.

"I'm working on it, Lena. I'm working on it." Throwing my arm over her shoulder, we make our way outside. She points out her Jeep, and we head that way. "Want to come over for dinner?"

She laughs. "No, thank you."

"How about we hang out after? Work on homework." I'm reaching here, but I'm not ready to let her go just yet.

"It's the first day of classes. We didn't have any homework."

"Never hurts to work ahead." We both know that I'm full of shit, but that's okay. She's smiling, so I'm taking that as a win.

"How about I'll see you tomorrow?" she suggests.

"That's a long time from now."

"You're going to be just fine." She surprises me when she raises up on her tiptoes and presses her lips to my cheek. "Thank you for today. You made it so much better than I thought it would be."

"That's how every day will be, Lena."

"We'll see." She opens up her car door. "I'll see you tomorrow, Stanley Riggins." She climbs into her Jeep and drives away. I stand here, like the lovesick fool that I am where she's concerned, and watch until I can no longer see her vehicle.

"What's up with you?" Roger asks.

"That's the girl I'm going to marry." I point to where Lena just disappeared down the road.

"What did you take?" he asks, concern lacing his voice.

"What?"

"You have to be on something. Come on, man, you're better than that."

I can't help it. My head falls back in laughter. "I didn't take anything. It's all about the magic, my man."

"Magic? Right?" he draws out. "Magic pussy, maybe," he mutters.

"Don't." My tone is stern. "Not with her. Don't go there."

He raises his hands in the air. "You do you, Riggins. All I'm saying is we're too young to be tied down. We need to taste all the flavors before we decide on our favorite."

"I already know my favorite. I'll catch you tomorrow," I say to my best friend, tossing my hand in the air. I make my way to my truck and head home.

"Finally!" I exclaim when my dad walks through the door from work.

"Talk about a welcome home." He chuckles. "What's up, kid?"

"Magic."

Dad tilts his head to the side and studies me. "What about it?"

"Not *it*. *Her*."

A slow smile tugs at his lips. "Her, huh?"

"All these years I thought you and Gramps were pulling my leg." I run my fingers through my hair. I didn't think he'd ever get home. I glance at the clock and see it's ten minutes after five. He's usually home at five. That was the longest ten minutes of my life. Okay, I'm exaggerating, but I needed to talk to him.

"All your eighteen years, huh?" he jokes.

"I'm being serious here, old man. She's... everything."

He nods. "Yeah, sounds about right."

"She thinks I'm crazy."

"That sounds about right too," he says. "You're going to have to tone it down, son. You can't scare her away. The magic, it's ours, but the women, you have to woo them still. It's not the same for them. This is a Riggins thing," he adds. "When we fall, we fall hard. I'm glad you're smart enough not to fight it. You're young, though. Are you sure?"

"Dad," I groan. "I'm positive. It's her. She's new in town, new to school. Her name is Lena, and she has dark hair and big blue eyes, and she's… her. She's mine."

"Then do right by her, Stanley. Never let a day go by that you don't tell her what she means to you. Well, actually, start out slow. Show her you're a man of your word. Be there for her and support her. I'm sure being new in town, this is all scary. Take your time, but be consistent. Show her what it means to be your magic."

"I told her all of that." I puff my chest out, proud that I got it right.

"Sounds to me like you've actually been listening when I thought you were letting my advice go in one ear and out the other." He smirks.

"I'm always listening, but I admit I thought it was all just two old men talking, trying to pull a fast one on me."

"I would never do that."

"Yes, you would." This time, I'm the one laughing. "But this magic you and Gramps keep talking about, I felt it. It's real. You're not crazy old men, after all," I tease.

"When do we get to meet her?" he asks.

"You just told me to take it slow."

"That doesn't mean you don't get to spend time with her. Besides, I should get to meet my future daughter sooner rather than later." He pauses, waiting for, I'm sure, a negative reaction from me.

He's not going to get one.

I'm young—just turned eighteen a couple of weeks ago—but there is nothing about the thought of Lena being my wife that scares me.

The magic is definitely real.

# CHAPTER *Lena* THREE

I T'S BEEN SIX months since I started my senior
year. Six months since meeting Stanley Riggins.
If you had asked me on that first day where I
would be six months later, I never would have
said in his arms, with the lights down low, in our
school gymnasium for our senior prom.

Stanley picked me up in his dad's truck. He was
wearing his black tux, with a purple tie and
cummerbund to match my dress. He had flowers
for me, and the first words out of his mouth were
"My girl is beautiful." My mom smiled as tears
welled in her eyes. She loves him, and his parents
love me. At least I'm pretty sure they do. They
treat me like family. The only thing missing is the
official title.

Stanley asked me on that first day to give him a chance. To let him prove he's a man of his word. He referred to me as his girlfriend, and I shut that title down immediately. I didn't know him well enough for him to claim that label. He asked for exclusivity to give him a chance, and I granted him that.

In the last six months, he's referred to me as his girl. Everyone in our school and our families assume we're officially boyfriend and girlfriend, but he's never mentioned it again since that very first day. I asked him to give me time, and he's done that.

As he holds me tightly in his arms as Journey's "Faithfully" blares through the speakers, I know in my heart that there is nothing more in this life I want than to be his. Tonight, after prom, we're all going to his place. His parents are hosting. We're camping out in the basement. It took his mom calling mine and assuring her we would be well supervised for my mom to agree. Not that she doesn't trust me, or Stanley, for that matter. We're both eighteen, so technically legal adults who will be graduating soon. It was more the principle of letting her daughter spend the night at a boy's house.

The song ends, and Stanley presses his lips to my forehead.

I tilt my head back to meet his eyes. "Want to get some fresh air?"

"Sure, baby."

That's something else. On day two, when I got to school, he was waiting for me in the parking lot. He said, "Good morning, baby." I didn't correct him, and now that's what he calls me. He doesn't care who's around to hear him. I learned that when he called me baby in front of his parents and my mom. My face heated, but Stanley didn't seem to mind the attention it gained him. He's unapologetically who he is, and to me, he's my safe place to land. This new school, my senior year, would have turned out a lot differently without him next to me.

With his arm around my waist, he pushes open the gym door, and we walk outside. The night air is cool but feels great against my heated skin. He pulls me into his arms, his front to my back, and presses his lips to my temple.

Tilting my head back against his shoulder, I stare up at the night sky. The stars look like millions of tiny diamonds against the inky blackness. "I've been thinking," I say, breaking the silence.

"About what, baby?"

"I want to ask you something."

"You can ask me anything. You know that."

I do know that, but I'm still nervous. I don't know why. I'm pretty certain what his answer will be. Swallowing back my nerves, I turn in his arms and clasp my hands behind his neck. I smile up at him as he locks his hands in a similar fashion at the small of my back.

"You're beautiful."

"You're a charmer."

"Only with you." He winks, and suddenly, my nerves are gone. This is a formality, one I'm not sure either of us needs, but I want it anyway.

"Stanley Riggins?"

"Baby." He kisses the tip of my nose.

"I want you to be mine."

"I am yours."

"Officially. I want you to be my boyfriend."

His eyes soften in the glow of the moonlight. "I've been yours since the moment I laid eyes on you."

I nod. We both know what he says is true. "We never talked about titles."

"I did. That first day."

"But I asked you to give me some time, and we haven't talked about it since."

He's smiling down at me as if I'm the greatest thing in his universe. It's a heady feeling to know there is someone who cares for me this deeply.

He moves his hands from the small of my back to my cheeks. His thumbs caress under my eyes. "Lena Hartford, one day to be Riggins—" He smirks. " —I love you completely and irrevocably."

My breath hitches. He's never said those words to me before. My heart races. I run my fingers through his hair to calm my nerves. "You love me?"

"You know I do, baby. You're my magic, but it's more than that. You're my heart and soul. We're going the distance, you and me. This is forever, Lena."

I swallow over the lump of emotion building in the back of my throat. "I love you too." My voice cracks. "My dad, he would have loved you. You know, I think he might have sent you to me. He knew I needed someone to lean on, to guide me through this year, and you were his pick."

His answer is to crush me in a hug, burying his face in my neck. I move my hands to wrap around his waist and hold on to him with everything I've got. I send up a silent thank-you to my father. I might not be a firm believer in the magic, as Stanley likes to call it, but I do believe my dad is watching over me, and he knew I needed this boy — no — this man in my life.

Stanley pulls away and bends, pressing his lips to mine. I open for him, and he leisurely explores my mouth. I'm putty in his hands as I lean into him, soaking up every moment. He slides his hand behind my neck and tilts my head just the way he wants me as he deepens the kiss. I lose all track of time. Nothing and no one exists but the two of us. His kisses are like a balm to my tattered heart, and they always make everything better. Then again, I think it's just Stanley. That's the effect he has on me.

"We should get you back inside." With his hand laced in mine, we head back to the gym to finish our senior prom. We both do so with the knowledge that no matter what happens after high school, we're going to experience it together.

"I'm so proud of you, sweetheart." My mom pulls me into her arms, crushing me in a fierce hug. "I wish he was here to see this," she whispers.

"Me too," I tell her as I retreat out of her embrace. "I'm glad that's over." I laugh, and Mom smiles.

Today is my high school graduation. It's hard to believe it's finally over. This year didn't turn out the way I thought it would. I thought I'd spend my senior year alone, lost in my heartache, but thanks to my incredible boyfriend and my new best friend, Gail, that's not what happened at all. I was sad, sure, but they both helped pull me from the darkness. It helped that my mom is also doing well and even getting out of the house with a few of her coworkers. We've picked up the pieces and are slowly putting them back together. Putting us back together.

"What's next?"

"I'm not sure." My eyes scan the gym for Stanley and his parents.

"Whatever you do, you'll be amazing. I think community college to start is a great idea."

"Yeah, at least until I decide what it is I want to do with my life. Did you always know?"

"No. It took me some time. I actually didn't want to go to college. Then, one day, I decided nursing was my calling. Your dad supported me with that decision. He worked two jobs, and I worked part time while I was in nursing school. We both did whatever we needed to do to make it happen." She wipes a tear from her eye as Stanley and his parents step up beside us.

"Congratulations, sweetie," his mom, Shelia, says, drawing me into a hug.

"You kept this one out of trouble this year. We thank you for that." His dad, Danny, chuckles. He's teasing, and we all know it. He takes his turn, hugging me before Stanley pulls me into his arms while our parents say hello.

"Now that we got that out of the way, we can start the next step," Stanley says, his voice low and only for me.

I turn to glance at him over my shoulder. "What's the next step?" I keep my voice barely above a whisper.

"We need to make you a Riggins." He winks, and I swear that action is tied to the flutter of my heart in some way.

"Let's figure out what we're going to do for careers, and then we can talk about changing names and all that." I don't know how I keep my voice even when there's a party of butterflies dancing inside my belly. I know we're young, but I've never been more certain than I am of the love I have for Stanley.

"That's not a no, baby." He's watching me, gauging my reaction.

"It's not a no," I agree. He grins.

With a nod from our parents, we make our way outside and head to Stanley's house. Neither Stanley nor I wanted a graduation party. Me, because I don't have family to invite, and him, well, honestly, I think it's because I'm not having one, but his parents were fine with the idea and insisted they host me and my mom for lunch.

"He only has eyes for you," Mom says. We're following Stanley and his parents to their place.

"He's a good guy." I don't know what else to say. Mom and I are close, but I've kept Stanley's talk of magic and how he told me on day one that I was his to myself. I'm aware that it sounded crazy as hell, and I didn't want her to worry about me more than she already was.

"His parents are nice as well."

"Yeah," I agree. Then I decide to bring up what I feel in my heart is true. "Sometimes, I think that Dad sent him to me. He knew I needed support outside of my mom for my senior year at a new school. He knew that I needed someone to heal my broken heart." I let the words hang, staring out the window, afraid of how Mom will react. I don't want to upset her before we get to the Riggins's house, but I've also been holding this in, and I'm curious about what she thinks.

"Your father was a good man, Lena. The best I've ever known. He was my best friend and the love of my life, and he loved you just as fiercely. I have no doubt that if he were able, he would have sent Stanley to you." Her voice cracks, and she clears her throat.

"Dad would have liked him."

"He would have loved him for you."

"Yeah? How do you know?" I love that we still talk about him, keeping his memory alive.

"Because Stanley looks at you the way your father used to look at me."

I let her words take root in my mind. Closing my eyes, I can see my parents in the kitchen making dinner after work. Dad would sing and dance and make every excuse in the book to touch my mom in some way. I smile as tears well in my eyes. I miss him so damn much.

"I love him." I blurt the words out. I've never said those words to my mom about Stanley. She's never asked, and well, I've just been keeping them to myself.

"I know you do."

"You and Dad were young too, right?"

"We were. We met the summer after high school graduation."

"I don't know what I want to do with my life. I don't know what career path I want to choose, but I do know that I'd really, really like for him to be by my side for whatever it is." Another honest truth that I've yet to speak out loud. I turn to watch her, seeing how she's aged since we lost Dad.

"Love is tough. It's a lot of hard work and compromise. Never take a single day with him for granted." She glances over at me. "Treat your relationship like the magical gift that it is, and you two will be just fine."

"Magical," I repeat. My heart flips in my chest. Stanley Riggins and his magic have changed my life.

"Definitely."

"I love you, Mom."

"Love you too, Lena."

We pull into the driveway, and I make a mental note to tell Stanley about our conversation later. Maybe there's something to his theory about the magic of love after all.

# CHAPTER *Stanley* FOUR

*Age Twenty, Community College Graduation*

**W**E DID IT. Lena and I both graduated with our associate's degrees. Mine is in business management, while hers is in accounting. Over the last year, we've talked a lot about what's next. Neither one of us really wanted to further our education to get our bachelor's degrees. We're both currently working in jobs we love and utilizing our education.

I was just promoted to dispatch at Nashville Concrete. The guys I work with like to give me shit because I'm young, and in their words, tied down to the old ball and chain, but they're a great group, and we all get along well despite our age difference.

Lena is working for the auditor's office, and she enjoys it. We're both using our degrees in our roles, and we're happy. We're also ready to start the rest of our lives together. That's why we signed a lease on a tiny one-bedroom apartment last night. Lena cried. Not because she doesn't want us to move in together but because she feels guilty for leaving her mom.

This has been hard for her. I might have put a little bug in my mom's ear, and she had a talk with Lena's mom, Lora. I knew that Lena would never bring it up on her own, and I know without a shadow of a doubt that Lora wants her daughter to keep moving forward. She understands that Lena won't live at home forever. That's all part of life.

When Lena called me this morning crying, I was ready to say the hell with graduation, but she assured me they were happy tears. She had a long heart-to-heart with her mom, and she's excited for us, just as I knew she would be.

That brings us to the present moment. This time, Lena and I insisted on hosting. We have nothing but paper plates, plastic forks, and cups because we just got our keys last night, but that's okay. This pepperoni and cheese pizza has never tasted better.

"I like what you've done with the place," Dad jokes.

"Right?" I play along. "We're thinking some lawn chairs over by the window will really liven the place up." I chuckle.

"Oh, don't forget the inflatable pool," Lena calls out from where she's standing in the small galley kitchen with our mothers.

"You know I'd never forget the pool," I call back to her. She blows me a kiss, and like the lovesick fool I am for her, I catch it and place my hand over my heart.

"How are you liking the magic?" Dad asks. I can hear the amusement in his voice.

"It's magical."

He tosses his head back in laughter. His hand comes down to rest on my shoulder. "I'm damn proud of you, son. You're going to do great things."

I turn to look at Lena. She's laughing at something my mom said. "She's the greatest."

"I won't argue with that, but I will let you in on a little secret." He pauses, and I know he's waiting for me to look at him.

"Dad, I believe you. The magic is real," I say, returning my gaze to his, giving him my full attention.

He nods. "Yeah, but it intensifies."

"I don't know how it could be any better than this. I have the love of my life in our home. We're starting our forever. It doesn't get better than that."

"Oh, it does. It gets better when she takes your last name. It gets better with each passing day that you wake up next to her. Then, one day, she's going to be carrying a piece of both of you. She's going to have your baby, Stanley, and when that happens—" Dad shakes his head. "It's a love like you've never known. Not just for her, but for your child."

"I don't think I could love her any more than I already do, Dad."

"You'll see." His eyes are on my mother, and there's a small smile tugging at his lips.

I used to think my dad and grandpa were just giving me shit. You know, like when they send you into the hardware store to ask for checkered paint. But I was wrong. So very wrong. I have no choice but to assume that he's going to be right about this as well.

I lock eyes with Lena and she smiles. I wink at her, and she blushes. I hope that never stops. I hope that when we're retired with a yard full of our kids and grandkids, I can still make her blush. Lord knows I'll never stop trying.

## One year post-graduation. Age Twenty-One

I always assumed that I wouldn't be nervous when I reached this point in my life. I thought I'd be confident if I found a woman I loved enough to want to spend the rest of my life with. I thought this part would be a breeze.

I assumed wrong.

I know Lena loves me. I'm not worried about that. I *am* confident in the love we share. It's the pressure of making this a moment she will always remember. I'm certain she's going to say yes. The love that we share is solid. If you ask my dad, it's the Riggins magic, and while I'm now a believer, I also know that it's us. It's who we are together. It's the love and respect we hold for one another.

That's the real magic.

I want to make all of her dreams come true. I want her to sit on our front porch with our grandbabies in her lap, telling them how Grandpa asked her to be his forever. We're young, but love doesn't know age. I know without a shadow of a doubt that she's it for me. Hell, I knew it the day I first laid eyes on her, our senior year. That's not going to change.

I look around our small apartment, making sure I have everything set. My future mother-in-law gave me her blessing and agreed to get Lena out of the apartment today so I could get everything set up.

Blowing out a heavy breath, I wipe my sweaty hands on my jeans and dim the lights. Moving to stand by the door, I wait. My heart races, the sound whooshing in my ears. Tapping my pocket, I feel the ring box. Everything is set, and in just a matter of minutes, Lena will be my fiancée.

I hear her keys in the door. I exhale and turn the knob before she can open it herself. "Welcome home, gorgeous." I lean in for a kiss before stepping back so she can enter the apartment. I quickly shut the door and move to stand before her in the small entryway — blocking the rest of the place from her view — and wrap her in a tight hug. "I missed you."

She laughs, and I swear that sound soothes my soul. "I missed you, too, but I was only gone a couple of hours." She holds up her hands, showing me her manicure. "I got the same color on my toes."

"Sexy," I say, kissing her again. I take a step back, and she moves with me.

"It's light pink. That's sexy?" She chuckles.

"*You* are sexy. So yes, if your fingernails and toenails are painted light pink, that's sexy too." I grin down at her as I continue to walk backward, leading her further into our apartment.

"Stanley Riggins, what am I going to do with you?" She shakes her head, a smile tugging at her lips.

This isn't how I planned it, but she gave me the perfect opening. Dropping to one knee, I reach into my pocket and pull out the ring box. My hands shake as I pull open the lid and present it to her.

"Marry me."

Her lips part as tears begin to well in her eyes.

"I had this big speech planned, and I was supposed to do this over there." I point behind me where the light pink—her favorite—and white balloon arch I spent the last two hours putting together awaits us. "But you asked what you were going to do with me, and well, I can't think of anything better than you taking my last name."

She sniffs, and her hands tremble as I present the ring to her.

"You're my entire world, Lena. Everything I am begins and ends with you. Will you do me the incredible honor of being my wife? Will you marry me?"

She's nodding before I'm finished. I pluck the ring from the cushion insert, toss the box to the side, and slip the round half-carat solitaire onto her finger. It's not much, but one day, I'll be able to upgrade her ring to one that shines just like she does. I don't have time to stand before she's bending down and crushing me in a hug. We fall back on the floor, and she straddles my hips. She's holding herself up with her hands pressed to my chest.

"I love you, Stanley Riggins."

"I love you too, future Mrs. Riggins."

Her lips crash with mine. I bury my hands in her hair, and she begins to rock her hips. My cock hardens. I want to tear our clothes off and sink inside her, but I know that I can't. This night, it was meant to be romantic. I have champagne and dinner that's warm in the oven, thanks to my mom's help.

"Slow down, baby."

She pulls her mouth from mine. Her chest is heaving with each breath she pulls into her lungs, and she's glaring at me. Desire swirls in her eyes, and it's killing me to stop this. "Stanley Riggins. I just agreed to be your wife."

"I know, baby." I smile up at her as I tuck her hair behind her ear so that I can see her face.

"Have you ever heard happy wife, happy life?"

I smile but quickly mask it because she's not smiling. "I want this to be a night you'll always remember. I had a plan."

"Plans change, Riggins." She gives me a pointed look. "What better way to celebrate me taking your name than being a part of me?"

"I'll always be a part of you. I'm supposed to romance you tonight." My cock knows what she's asking for. I want her. I always want her, and I know what her pussy feels like when she's milking my cock, but I had plans. I wanted to romance her and take things slow. My future wife didn't seem to get that memo.

"Fine."

She moves off me, and I swear my cock weeps at the loss of her heat, even through our clothes. She lies on the floor next to me and spreads her arms out wide. "Have your way with me. Show me what you got, Riggins."

"I have dinner and champagne."

"But I want this. I want you."

There is nothing I won't give her, and if this is the memory she wants, it's the one I want to give her. I lie back on the floor and spread my arms out like hers. "This is your show, baby."

She grins. It's a little devilish as she rushes to straddle my hips once more. "Are you sure you're ready to be at my mercy?" she taunts.

Lifting my hand, I rest my palm against her cheek. "Forever." Her eyes soften, and she gives me a quick kiss before climbing to her feet. "I'm gonna need you naked, Riggins."

I can't hide my grin. "Yes, ma'am."

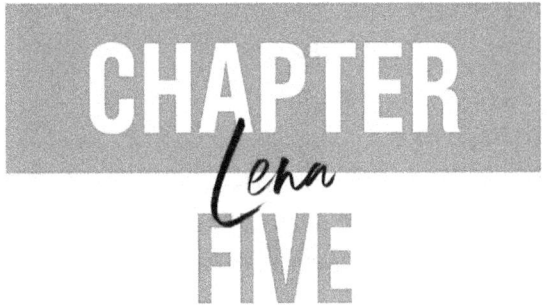

# CHAPTER
*Lena*
# FIVE

**S**TANLEY SCRAMBLES TO his feet and pulls his shirt over his head, tossing it to the floor. He smirks when my heated gaze washes over his abs.

"You see something you like, baby?"

"Meh." I shrug, and he lunges forward, making me scream and rush away from him.

"Why am I the only one getting naked, future Mrs. Riggins?" he asks, sliding his jeans over his muscular thighs.

"Oh, you mean you want me to strip too?" I tease.

"Lena," he growls. The sound goes straight to my core.

"I'm definitely going to need you naked, future Mrs. Riggins." His eyes smolder as he tosses my earlier words back at me.

"Like this?" I lift my shirt, pulling it over my head and casually letting it fall to the floor at my feet.

"That's a start."

"Oh, so I should do this too?" I reach for the button of my jeans and slowly unbutton and lower the zipper. I exaggerate, wiggling my hips to lower the jeans, kicking them off once they fall to my ankles.

"I'm a lucky bastard," he mumbles, taking a step toward me.

"Uh uh uh." I lift my hand to stop him. "This is my show, remember?"

He raises his hands in the air, a crooked smile on his lips. "I'm watching."

"My mercy," I remind him.

He nods.

Turning, I give him my back. I pull my hair to one side over my shoulder and bend over. He groans, and the sound only fuels me to tease him further. I do a little shimmy and shake of my hips before slowly lowering my panties.

"Fuck," he rasps when they reach my thighs. "Baby." Need burns in his voice.

Standing to my full height, I kick my panties to the side and turn to face him. He has his hard cock in his hand, and he's squeezing. "Does it hurt?" I watch as he strokes his tight fist up and down his length.

He nods. His eyes are filled with desire as he rakes them over me. "I need you."

"Hmmm." I tap my index finger against my chin. "Maybe I could try to make it better?" I take a step closer. "Oh, but I'm not naked yet." I bite down on the inside of my cheek when his breathing accelerates. I stop just a few feet before him, just out of arm's length.

Reaching behind me, I unclasp my bra and make a slow production of peeling down one strap, then the other, before letting it fall to my feet.

"So fucking beautiful," he murmurs.

"Mr. Riggins, I think you should sit down." I nod toward the couch. He steps toward me and wraps his arms around my waist, lifting me from the floor. I squeal, holding on around his neck as he carries us to the couch. He slowly lowers me to the cushioned seat and hovers over me. "My show," I remind him.

"Do your worst." He stands and holds his arms out at his sides.

"Can you maintain that pose?" I ask him, sitting up and licking my lips. Reaching out, I fist his hard cock, and he moans. "Can you stand with your arms at your sides and let me have my fun?"

I peer up at him in time to see his throat bob as he swallows. "I can try," he grits out as I tighten my grip with each stroke.

"What about if I do this?" Leaning forward, I run my tongue over the tip of his cock, tasting him.

His arms start to drop, but he quickly lifts them back in the air out to his sides. I pull away and smirk up at him. "I don't care where you put your hands, but you can't touch me."

"Lena," he groans, and I can feel the wet heat pool between my thighs.

"Those are the rules."

"I'm supposed to be making love to you." His voice is soft, but there's still a layer of underlying lust in his tone.

Lifting my hand, I gaze at my engagement ring. "I know you love me, Stanley."

"More than anything," he's quick to reply.

"Tonight will be one that I'll always remember. The night you asked me to be yours forever. I want it to be memorable for you too."

"It is. You said yes, baby. What could be more memorable than that?"

I smirk. "I'll show you."

His eyes soften, and my heart swells. This man, he swooped in and stole my heart when I least expected him, and now, I can't imagine my life without him.

"I love you." My voice cracks with my overwhelming love for him. It's large and loud, and it's everything I never knew that I needed.

"Lena, I love you too." He reaches for me but stops before his hand touches my face. "This is going to be difficult."

I smile up at him. "It's going to be fun." To prove my point, I take him into my mouth. I don't stop until his length hits the back of my throat.

"Son-of-a…" His voice trails off when I let him fall from my lips.

"Something wrong?"

"Let me touch you."

I stand and nod toward the couch. "Sit." He does as I ask, immediately falling to the cushion and peering up at me with hooded eyes. As I reach for a pillow for my knees, he grabs a hold of it, stopping me.

"I'm not coming down your throat, Lena. Not tonight."

I nod, release my grip on the pillow, and straddle his hips on the couch. His hands hover at my waist, but he doesn't touch me.

"This is so much better," I say, digging my fingers into his shoulders as I rock my hips. My core rubs over his hard cock, and this time, we both moan in anticipation.

"Let me touch you."

"I'm touching you," I counter, and he groans. "What if I do this?" Reaching between us, I grip his cock and lift up on my knees. I position him at my entrance and slowly slide down until he's buried deep inside me. "How's that?" I ask, my voice breathless.

"Heaven."

I smile at him. "What about this?" I lift up on my knees and slide back down.

"Torture. Pure fucking torture."

"I don't know, feels pretty good to me." Closing my eyes, I tilt my head back and cup my breasts as I focus on slowly lifting and lowering myself onto him.

"Nipples," he grates.

I open my eyes. "What?"

"Pinch your nipples." He licks his lips as his eyes are laser focused on my breasts.

I do as he asks, and I don't try to stop the moan of pleasure that falls from my lips. I grind my hips, taking what I need from him.

"Lena?"

"Yeah?" I ask, my eyes closed, letting the thousands of sensations of feeling him inside me and the tug on my nipples wash over me. He curses under his breath, which has me opening my eyes and meeting his stare.

"Let. Me. Touch. You." He bites his words out through gritted teeth as he fists his hands at his sides. His eyes snap to mine, and the hunger I see takes my breath away.

"Hands on my hips," I concede.

"Thank fuck." He immediately grips my hips. His hold is tight, and his jaw is clenched. He lifts me and slams me back down without notice. I gasp, but it doesn't seem to break through this fog he's captured in.

"S—Stanley," I call out his name. Why I thought him not touching was a good idea, I'll never know.

"I'm here, baby," he replies as he continues to lift me and slam me back down on him. It's wild and intense and absolutely perfect.

"More. Please—" I don't even know what I'm asking for. All I know is that I want more of it. More of his tight grip on my waist, more of his hard length inside me.

I want it all.

Anything and everything he's got to give me.

I'll take it.

"Tell me I can move my hands, Lena." It's a demand, one that I'm happy to give in to.

"Yes. Yes. Please, yes!" I call out. Suddenly his hands are everywhere. I take over, bouncing on my knees as he cups my breasts.

Why does it feel so much better when he's the one squeezing my nipples?

"Your pussy is going crazy, baby," he says, sliding his hand behind my neck and pulling me into a kiss. I slow my actions because I'm ready to come, and I don't want to, not yet. Not without him. Instead, I grind on him, sensually rocking my hips while his tongue explores my mouth.

When he pinches my nipple with his free hand, I clench around him.

"I'm not gonna last long if you keep doing that."

As if I'm a puppet to his words, I squeeze around him again.

"Fuck," he grits. "Need you there," he breathes against my lips. He slides his hand that was tweaking my nipple between us. His thumb finds my clit, and I rock my hips faster. Grind harder.

"There you go," he praises. "Take what you need, baby. I'm so close."

"S—St..." My voice trails off as the most intense orgasm of my life takes over my body. I feel the burning tingle race down my spine, settling between my thighs.

"Fuck, so tight," he says through gritted teeth before he holds my hips still and releases inside me.

I'm a limp noodle as I fall to his chest, and he wraps his arms tightly around me. We're both trying to catch our breath. He's pulsing inside me.

Then again, maybe that's me. It's hard to tell where he ends and I begin at this point.

"That was… mind-blowing." He kisses my temple.

It takes extreme effort to lift my head, but I manage to do so. I also raise my hand and wiggle my ring finger, causing my engagement ring to sparkle. Exhilaration takes over as I process tonight's events. We're getting married. My heart thumps wildly inside my chest, and excitement courses through my veins. I'm marrying my best friend. "How does this change things? It did, right? That wasn't just me who felt like it was an out-of-body experience?"

He grins, his eyes sparkling. "It's the magic, baby."

I can't help it. I laugh. It's not that I don't believe in this Riggins magic that the men in his family seem to go on and on about, but whenever something incredible happens, he gives all the credit to the magic.

As for me, I won't disagree that it's magical, but it's magic we make together. It's the two of us forever, and that's what makes it special.

# CHAPTER

## *Stanley*

## SIX

"**I** THINK IT could work," I tell my fiancée. It's Friday night, and we're having dinner in our apartment, and I've just dropped a bomb on her. Okay, not a bomb per se, but definitely something I know she wasn't expecting from me.

I want to start my own business. I'd, of course, keep my full-time job, but this is something I've been thinking about for weeks now. Ever since my work decided to sell an old box truck last week. They pulled it out front and slapped a For Sale sign on it, and my mind has been racing with ideas ever since.

I've been working for the concrete company since starting college, and I've learned a lot. Especially that logistics is a growing business. I've been listening and watching, and we get calls on the daily for suggestions for trucks, freight, or even just moving tools and equipment. That's where I would come in.

It would be hard only doing it on evenings and weekends, which will be time that I'll be losing with Lena unless she comes with me, but my gut is telling me that this is the right move for me. For us. For our family and our future.

"Let me make sure I understand. We buy the box truck and spend our evenings and weekends moving things for other people?" She wrinkles her brow — something she does when she's concentrating. She's not blowing off the idea. She's giving it actual consideration, and I love her even more for it. I need her on board with this. This might be my idea, but it's our joint savings that we were hoping to use for a down payment on a house. It's not all of it, but a nice chunk.

"To start, yes. We could move equipment for businesses or deliver products for businesses as well. Whatever they need as long as it will fit in the truck safely. Logistics is a huge, growing business. I think we can make a lot of extra cash this way. We could get out of this apartment and into a house sooner than expected. We could start our family," I tell her.

Her eyes sparkle on that last part. I know Lena wants to be a mom, and I want to give her that and so much more. I want to lay the world at her feet. I truly feel this is the path I need to take to do that.

"How much is the truck?" she asks.

At least she hasn't shot down the idea yet. "It's old and doesn't look like much. The plant manager said they would sell it to me for four thousand since I'm an employee."

"Okay. What about insurance? Business insurance?" she asks. "What about gas and maintenance? Is it in decent shape? Is it going to nickel and dime us and eat up the potential profits?"

Damn, she's on top of this. I love that she's taking this wild ride with me. "I called to check on the insurance, and it's not much. We can pay it monthly and use the profits. It's in excellent condition. Barry, our mechanic, kept up with it. It doesn't look like much, but it runs like a well-oiled machine. Gas would be included in the freight charge with each load. We'd figure that in and charge the customer accordingly so it doesn't cut into our profits." I carefully answer each of her questions. It's important to look at every angle and assess the good and the bad before diving into this new business venture.

"Where are we going to park it?" she asks, scrunching up her nose again. "We only get two spots here at the apartment complex."

"I'd keep it at my parents' place until we move." That's the end goal. Get out of this apartment and get into a house where we can raise our kids. A yard for them to run and play in. It's her dream, mine too, and I'm going to work my ass off for it to come true.

"And where do you plan to find clients for this... logistics service you want to offer?" Lena stands and begins to gather our plates and carries them to the kitchen. I trail along behind her. We rinse them off together and load the dishwasher as we clean up from dinner. This has become our nightly routine, and it's my favorite because it's my time with her. It doesn't matter what we're doing. We're together. That's what matters.

"Advertising, word of mouth, and we have people call the plant all the time asking for numbers of people who can haul things. I know they would give them our information."

"Your information. I can't drive that big old box truck." She laughs.

"*Our* information. This is our business, Lena. It might have been my idea, and I might be the one doing the driving and heavy lifting, but this is ours, baby. I won't do it any other way."

I watch as she dries her hands before she turns to face me. "You want this? You really want to try?" She tilts her head to the side to study me. I don't know what she's looking for in my expression, but I hope she can see how determined I am for this to work for us.

"I do. I know we can do this, Lena. It's the extra income that will get us into our dream home."

She smiles. "You're my home, Stanley."

I can't take it a minute longer. I pull her into my arms and twirl her in circles in our small galley kitchen. Her laughter fills the air surrounding us, and I soak up every second of it. Our kitchen is barely big enough for this, but we make it work.

When we finally stop spinning, I wait for her to look up at me. "You're my home, too, baby, but I want more for us and for our kids."

Her eyes soften, just as they do every time I mention us starting a family. "We're not even married yet," she teases.

"We will be, and we will have a family, and I want to be able to give you all everything." I hold her gaze so she can see how much this means to me. Not just this side hustle I want to embark on, but providing for my family.

"We just need you."

I smile when she says we. I don't even know if she realizes that's what she said. It's crazy of me to get so excited about her referring to us having kids, but this is what I want. A life with her. One we build together.

Her words have my heart flopping around in my chest. We need to set a wedding date soon. "I know." I do know. That doesn't mean I don't want to give them more. I know I can make this business go. It might not make me a millionaire, but it will be a good side hustle to bring in some extra cash. We both do well. We're not hurting for money, but we're not swimming in it either. Houses and kids are expensive.

I know we can do this.

She peers up at me under long lashes. She doesn't speak for several long heartbeats and worry gnaws at me that she's going to say it's not the right time. Her hands that were holding on around my neck, move to rest against my cheeks.

"I'm with you, Stanley Riggins. Always. If you want this, we'll do it. We'll take the money out of savings and buy the truck."

"If it fails, it sets us back for a house."

Dad always says open and honest communication is everything in a relationship. While I know I can make this work, and I'll give it everything I've got, it's only right to mention that I could be wrong, and this idea will be a bust. I really don't think that will happen, but it's responsible to look at both sides of the coin when making huge life decisions.

My fiancée shrugs. "You're my home. I told you that. If this sets us back, then it does. We'll handle it together."

"I promise you I'll work my ass off to make our money back and so much more. My gut tells me this is a good move for us, baby."

"I don't know much about what you want to do, but I can run numbers and keep track of costs and invoicing that kind of thing. I'll do whatever I can to help you succeed."

"*Us* succeed." I kiss the corner of her mouth.

"Us." She grins.

"I love you." Those three words aren't enough to explain the depths of what I feel for her, but it's the best I've got at the moment.

She lifts up on her toes and presses her lips to mine. "I love you too. Now, let's take a drive to look at this truck." She pulls away and moves to slip into her shoes. She grabs her purse and goes to stand by the front door. "Ready?"

"Yes." I take her hand in mine and lead her out to my truck.

On the way to the plant, we talk about advertising and things we'll need, like flyers and business cards. Lena even suggested an ad in the local paper. She offered to go door to door to local businesses to pass out flyers. She's one-hundred-percent behind me, and that's got me feeling some sort of way. It has my chest so full it feels as though it might explode with gratitude and love.

I'm going to make this work. I'm going to make this a success, not for me, but for her, for us, and for our future children.

This is going to work.

# CHAPTER
*Lena*
## SEVEN

*Age Twenty-Two*

**M**Y HEART HAS a heaviness, but it also feels light as a feather. I know that's contradicting, but let me explain.

Today is my wedding day.

The heaviness is from missing my father. He was supposed to be here with me today. It was supposed to be him who walked me down the aisle to the man I love. I'm missing him so much, and I know my mom is too. She's taking his place. She's walking me down the aisle. I was so worried about asking her, but with Stanley's encouragement, I did it. It's not that I was worried she would say no. I didn't want to cause her more pain. He was the love of her life, and I know she misses him terribly every single day. I do, too, but knowing the love I have in my heart for Stanley, I can't imagine the pain my mother has been dealing with since we lost Dad.

So yeah, there is a heaviness that sits on my chest, but the light-as-a-feather parts keep it from pulling me under with the pain of missing him. I'm marrying the love of my life. A man who took one look at me and knew I was meant to be his. A man who has never wavered in his devotion to me. A man who wants to give me his last name and build a life with me. A man I know, without a shadow of a doubt, my father would not only approve of, but he would have loved him as the son he never had. Of that, I'm certain.

"Your father would have loved him," my mom says as if she can read my thoughts.

"I think so too." I meet her watery gaze, the one that matches my own in the mirror as she stands behind me with her hands on my shoulders.

"You look beautiful, Lena. The most beautiful bride I've ever seen."

"Present company excluded," I tease.

She smiles and shakes her head. "Your father would have said something similar, I'm sure." She smiles. The pain of missing him is present in everything we do, but so is the love that we had for him and him for us. He's here today with us. We both know it, even if we don't say it.

"Yeah," I agree, dabbing a tissue under my eye, trying to salvage my makeup.

"I'm so proud of you, Lena."

"I love you, Mom."

"I love you too." She clears her throat. "Now, let's get you married. I'm sure Stanley is pacing at the altar."

"I'm not late."

She smiles. "Daughter dearest, the way he loves you—you could be twenty minutes early to the altar, and he would be there waiting."

I laugh. "That's a little much."

"Do you not know the man you're marrying?" she jokes.

Before I can reply, there's a knock at the door. "Come in," I call out. My future in-laws step into the room. They both rush to give me a hug and tell me how beautiful I look.

"Thank you," I say, trying to fight my tears.

"Did he send you?" my mom asks. There's amusement in her tone.

"We were headed to see our girl before, but yeah. He's at the altar and has been for the last thirty minutes," his mom confesses.

"But we still have fifteen minutes before the ceremony starts." Even with my argument, I know

Stanley. I know he wants this. I know he wants nothing more than for me to take his last name. This has been a long time coming. We're both more than ready to start the next phase of our lives together.

My future father-in-law grins. "He's just ready to marry you, Lena."

I glance at my mom, and she's wearing a smug grin.

"Told you so."

Stanley's parents laugh, and after another round of hugs, they leave, and it's just Mom and me again.

"You've found a love that most search for their entire lives. Embrace it, and him. He might be anxious, but it's not because he thinks you're not going to show. He just wants you to be his wife."

"I love him so much."

She smiles. "I know you do. Come on, let's go calm your groom's nerves and get you married."

With my arm linked through my mother's, we make our way out of the room and head toward the double doors of the church that will lead me to Stanley. She gives my arm a gentle squeeze as the doors are pulled open. My gaze goes straight to the altar where he's waiting for me.

His head pops up, and he freezes. With every step I take to get closer to him, my heart pounds in my chest. I'm about to be Mrs. Stanley Riggins, and all I can think is it's about damn time.

When we arrive at the altar, he steps forward and reaches for me, but my mom holds up her hand, and all the guests laugh. She doesn't get to say anything before Stanley leans in and kisses her cheek.

"I'll love her with everything I have until the end of time."

My gaze is glued to him as he looks my mother in the eye. I hear her sniff, and my own tears burn in the back of my throat.

"I know you will," my mom tells him. "Welcome to the family, Stanley."

He swallows hard. "Thank you."

Mom turns to me and kisses my cheek. "Love you," she whispers and steps back.

Stanley swoops in and takes my hands in his. "Love you," he mouths.

"Who here gives this woman away?" the minister asks.

"She's a strong, independent woman," my mom says, her voice loud and clear. "However, her late father and I do."

I smile as I lose my battle with tears. I should have assumed she'd mention Dad. I watch her as she walks to her seat. Next to her is a picture of my father in the seat that should have been his. My eyes leak with tears, and I pull my gaze back to Stanley.

"He's here, baby."

"I love you." My voice cracks, but it's also loud enough for everyone to hear.

"That's good, wife. That's real good because I love you too. Now, let's change your name, yeah?"

I nod, unable to find my voice through my tears. Stanley leans in and kisses the tip of my nose. I shudder a breath and square my shoulders. I give him another nod, which he returns with a panty-melting smile.

The minister welcomes everyone and begins to talk about marriage and love. I'm trying to listen to him, but I'm finding it difficult. Stanley has my hands in his, and his thumbs keep tracing over my knuckles. His gaze hasn't left mine, not once.

"Now, the bride and the groom have prepared their own vows."

"Lena." Stanley clears his throat. His eyes mist with tears, and my heart melts. "I love you." The guests laugh. "I don't know if it's magic. I don't know if it's a higher power, but whatever brought you to me, I will forever be grateful. My love for you was instant and the most real thing I've ever felt. We took our time. We let that love grow, we nurtured it, and here we are. Forever isn't long enough with you. I'll love you this lifetime and all of the next. I promise to be your partner. I want to be your shoulder on the bad days, and I want to revel in your happiness on the good days. My heart and soul are yours, and I can't wait to see what we do next."

I exhale and try to get my tears under control. "I love you too." I take a moment to find my words. "You came into my life when I was floating. I needed a safe place to land, and you offered me that. You're not only the love of my life. You're my best friend. I will be your partner and walk beside you through whatever life sends our way. I know you're going to do amazing things, and I'm honored that I get to share those wins with you. There will be losses, and I'll be there for those too. For every second of our forever, I want to be your safe place to land. I'm honored to call you my husband, and I know that wherever life takes us, it's going to be a journey filled with love and happiness." I repeat his words back to him, "My heart and soul are yours, and I can't wait to see what we do next."

He leans in and kisses me. "I love you so damn much, Mrs. Riggins."

"We're not there yet, son," the minister jokes.

"Can we get there?" Stanley asks. His voice is strong, and the love shining in his eyes would have me falling to my knees if he didn't have a tight grip on my hands.

"The rings?" the minister asks.

"Yeah, we're gonna need those," Stanley says, and the guests laugh again.

I smile at him as he turns and accepts my ring.

"Repeat after me," the minister instructs. We each take our turn and take our vows, before sliding the white-gold bands onto our fingers.

"Now, you may kiss your bride."

"Finally." Stanley expels a heavy breath, sliding his arm around my waist and hauling me into his chest.

When his lips touch mine, sparks fly just as they always do. Only this time, it's different. It's more because I know that he's my husband. I know that no matter where life takes us, he'll be by my side, and there is nothing in this world that I want more than that.

Slowing the kiss, Stanley rests his forehead against mine. "My wife," he murmurs.

"My husband."

"Fuck, I love that. Say it again."

"I love you, husband."

"Mrs. Riggins, you are my world." He kisses me again, not showing an ounce of care that our friends and family are watching us. In this moment, there's just the two of us.

# CHAPTER
## *Stanley*
# EIGHT

I CAN'T TAKE my eyes off my wife as she lies beside me in a white, barely there bikini. It's day three of our honeymoon and my wife decided today we needed some fresh air. The last two days we've been holed up in our suite.

When we talked about our honeymoon, Lena said she wanted to stay semi close to home since we'd be spending the majority of our time in the suite.

In bed.

Wrapped around one another.

She wasn't wrong.

The only other thing she said was that she'd like white sand and blue water. That's how we landed here, in Clearwater Beach, Florida. We are staying at a hotel on the beach in a suite that has a balcony with a clear view of the blue water my wife requested.

My wife.

Damn if it doesn't feel good to call her that. The last two days have been more than I could have expected. I carried her over the threshold, stripped her bare, and that's how we spent the next forty-eight hours. The only clothing we even bothered to put on were the robes that were provided by the hotel. Until today.

That brings us to now. Sitting on the beach, soaking up the rays, and having a nice cold drink. Lena read for a little bit while I just sat here and enjoyed the view. The ocean view wasn't bad either.

Taking another peek at my wife — because let's face it, I can't take my eyes off her — I see her skin pinking from the sun. "Baby." Reaching over, I gently trace my hand over her back. "You're going to burn. It's time for more sunscreen."

"I'm too comfy," she grumbles.

"Come on, lazybones."

"Fine, but I'm cooling off in the water first." She sits up, adjusts her skimpy-ass bikini top to make sure her assets are covered, tosses her sunglasses onto the chair beside her, and stands. She takes off running for the ocean, and I scramble to my feet to chase after her.

I will always chase after her.

We crash into the water at the same time. Wrapping my arms around her waist, I lift her high, and let us both fall back into the waves. After we've both come up for air, she turns and wraps her arms and legs around me.

"You're beautiful, Mrs. Riggins."

"I'm a sure thing." She laughs. "You don't need to work so hard. This proves that." She lifts her left hand from where it was locked behind my neck and wiggles her engagement ring and wedding band. The diamond glitters beneath the rays of the Florida sun.

Leaning in, I kiss her. It's a soft press of my lips to hers, but it ignites a fire inside me, just the same as if it were hot and feverish. I take my time, slowly trailing my tongue across her lips. She opens for me, like the queen that she is, and I slide my tongue against hers. I explore her mouth with languid strokes.

Her legs clamp around my waist, and she grinds her bikini-covered pussy over my cock.

"Stanley." My name is a plea from her lips, one I relish to hear every day for the rest of my life. I smile against her lips because this is my life. My wife in my arms, kissing her, holding her anytime I want.

This is my happy place.

Not the beach.

The woman.

My wife.

She grinds down on me again as her fingernails dig into my scalp. Moving my hands from the backs of her thighs, I slide them beneath her bikini bottoms and grip her ass cheeks, helping guide her over my cock.

"There are people watching."

"They can't see what we're doing."

She laughs. It's a musical sound. My favorite sound. "I'm sure they can make the correct assumption."

"You ready to head back to the room?"

"Yes. We've had enough fresh air for one day." She kisses me quickly before pulling out of my arms and I let her. She starts to swim toward the shore but stops when she realizes I'm not following her. "What's wrong?"

"Baby, if I walk out of this water right now, there will be no guessing what was going on out here beneath the waves." This earns me more of her magical laughter, which does nothing to quell the beast in my shorts.

Closing my eyes, I think of work. I let my mind go to everything that's going on and what I'll have to do when I get back from this week in paradise with my new wife. Eventually, my hard-on dies down enough for me to leave the water.

Once we're back on shore, she takes my hand and leads me to our lounge chairs. We gather our things, tossing them into a tote bag that I throw over my shoulder before making our way back to the hotel.

In the elevator up to our room, there's another couple with us. My wife backs up into me, rubbing her ass over my cock. I grip her hips, but the minx does it again. When I realize that the couple is on our same floor, I want to groan in frustration. As soon as the doors slide open, I grab Lena by the hand and race down the hall to our room. I don't care what it looks like to the other couple. I need my wife.

As soon as the door to our suite slams shut, I push Lena's back up against it and kiss the breath from her lungs. The tote bag over my shoulder falls to the floor as I grip her ass, lifting her against the wall.

"I need you."

"Yeah?" She rocks her hips.

Reaching between us, I manage to slide my swim trunks down and free my cock. With quick movements, I push Lena's bikini bottoms to the side, and slide into her. She's wet, just as I knew she would be, and so fucking tight. I've been inside her more times than I can count, and double that since we've been on our honeymoon. But every fucking time feels like the first with her. Her wet tight pussy grips me like a vise, and I'm barely holding on.

"Whatever you need to do to get there, I need you to do it. I'm ready to fucking come, but I won't do it without you." Her pussy convulses, and I grin. "You feel that, baby? The way your pussy is milking my cock?"

She moans. It's a sound filled with need and desire. Her fingers are buried in my hair, and she tugs, causing a smarting of pain, but I welcome it. It fuels me to bring us both over the edge of ecstasy.

I thrust my hips faster, quick short movements that I know will take us both where we want to go. "Take off your top," I tell her. I need to feel her hard nipples against my skin. She does as I say while I continue to push inside her. When her tits pop free, I stop to take one into my mouth. She lifts herself off me and slowly lowers, and the slow delicious friction causes her pussy to squeeze my cock even tighter.

I suck harder, giving her breasts equal amounts of my attention. "Babe." Her voice is throaty and sexy as hell.

She's close.

"Tell me you're there, wife. Tell me your pussy is ready to drench my cock."

"I—I'm there."

"Good. Now hold on. I'm going to fuck you hard and fast, but I promise I'll make love to you next."

"Hard and fast. That. Let's do that." She's nodding as I lean in and kiss her. I take my time slowly lifting her and pulling her back down on my cock. I have to force myself to stop kissing her so I can do what I promised and fuck her.

"Ready, baby?"

"Stop teasing me and fuck me already!" she says, frustrated. She's right on the edge. I can feel it in the way her body is responding. I can see it with each ragged breath she drags into her lungs, and then there's her eyes. They're swimming with lust.

"Hold on." She barely has time to lock her arms around my neck before I'm pumping into her hard and fast. She buries her head in my neck as I race to take us both to the release we've been craving.

"Come!" I demand.

"Yes. Yes. Yes," she pants as she finally lets go. It's more than I can take as I spill inside her.

We stand here, her back against the door, my body holding her there as we try to catch our breath. We're clinging to one another like we need to do so to live, and that's pretty much how I feel. The need that I have for her is beyond anything I've ever felt. It's magical, and all-consuming, and I wouldn't have it any other way.

# CHAPTER
*Lena*
## NINE

*Age twenty three*

S O MUCH HAS happened in the last year. Stanley and I got married and just celebrated our first wedding anniversary. It doesn't seem like a year could have passed already, but here we are. We've been enjoying our time together as husband and wife. We make it a point to find time for one another, even with our busy schedules and Stanley's business.

His business has taken off to something I never could have expected. Today, we're expanding yet again. We started with one small box truck, and now we have four box trucks and two semis.

The side hustle he wanted to start has turned into a full-blown business. I'm so damn proud of him. It brings tears to my eyes. He's worked tirelessly to make this happen, and during it all, there was never a time I didn't feel like the most important person in his life.

It's also allowed for us to start looking for a house. It's time for us to move out of the apartment we've called home for the last couple of years. The tiny space has served us well, but we're ready for more. Ready for what comes next, and right now, that's a house of our own on the outskirts of the city.

Pulling my car up to the house, I see Stanley's truck in the driveway. I park behind him and climb out of the car. He comes rushing toward me, a huge smile on his face.

"I missed you, wife," he says, kissing me softly.

"I missed you too." It's only been since before we left for work this morning since I've seen him—not days—but you would never be able to tell. This is how he always greets me whenever we've spent any amount of time apart.

And the wife part, yeah, we're just over a year into our marriage, and he still likes to refer to me as "wife." I don't object because I like it. I like being reminded I'm his, and I refer to him as "husband" just as much. One, because I know he likes it, and two, it feels good to remind the universe that this incredible man is mine, all mine.

"So, what do you think?" He keeps one arm wrapped around me while the other gestures toward the house. "It's three bedrooms, two and a half baths, and has a decent-sized yard."

"It's beautiful and so much bigger than our apartment," I tell him as I stare up at the two-story house. "Can we afford this?" I'm mentally crunching the numbers. I know that we can. We've talked about it at length, but buying a home is not only a huge investment but a big step for our family.

"Baby, we've talked about this. Even taking the twenty percent down payment from our savings leaves us a nice little nest egg."

"I know." I nod. "I'm just… this is happening so much sooner than we thought it would. We had a five-year plan, and this wasn't until the end of that."

He grins. "We're kicking ass, baby."

I laugh, hiding my face in his chest. "*You're* kicking ass," I say, peering up at him.

"Nope. We're a team, Lena Riggins. There is no me without you. You've been there every step of the way. We've built this business. It's ours, baby."

I know he's right, but really, I've just been there to support him. Sure, I do the books, but the business has grown so much that he now has an accounting team that takes care of it all. Either way, I know not to argue with him about it. In Stanley's eyes, we're partners in everything we do. No matter if I had a hand in it or not.

"Can we go inside?" I ask, instead of debating with him.

"Yeah, we can. The realtor is already in there. I asked her to give us a few minutes."

I grin up at him, not able to hide my enthusiasm. "I'm excited." I pull out of his embrace, lace my fingers through his, and guide us to the front door.

We walk inside into a small foyer with a set of steps. To the left of the steps is a sitting room, and to the right is the half bath. As we explore further, the laundry room is just off to the right, which leads to the attached garage, and a little farther down the hall is the kitchen. To the left is a dining room, and to the right is a larger living room with a fireplace. All three bedrooms and two bathrooms are upstairs.

I've studied the pictures and the layout on the realtor's site more times than I should be admitting. Partly because of my excitement and partly because it's a huge deal to buy a house. I want to make sure we think of all aspects of what our growing family will be like.

We take our time walking hand in hand through each room. We point out things like having family dinners in the dining room, to turning the second living room area into an office for Stanley.

"*Our* office. In fact, we could put two desks right there on that wall, side by side."

"I don't need a home office."

"But I could use one, and I want you with me so—" He shrugs.

"What am I going to do with you?"

"Love me."

"With my whole heart." I rise up on my toes and kiss him softly.

"What do you think?" he asks, wrapping his arms tightly around me, keeping me pressed to his chest.

"I think that this place feels like home."

"Me too, Mrs. Riggins. Let's go talk to the realtor and put in an offer."

*Two months later.*

"I'm never moving again," I declare as I plop down on the couch next to my husband. We just unpacked the last box in our new home. "How in the world did we get all of that stuff in our tiny apartment?"

He laughs and pulls me onto his lap. "Next time, we'll hire movers." He kisses my temple.

"Movers are expensive."

"We can afford it. Besides, if we got that much stuff in our apartment, can you imagine after living here for a few years?"

"This is it, Riggins. We're never moving again."

"Okay, baby," he says.

I know he's agreeing with me because I'm worn out and exhausted. I don't know why I've been so tired lately. It's as if I can barely keep my eyes open.

"Why don't you go upstairs and shower? I'll order us some pizza and run to town to pick it up."

"You really do love me," I tease.

"Yes." He kisses me softly. "I'll be back in twenty." He stands and moves toward the kitchen to make the call. "I'll be back!" he calls out.

I hear the garage door open and close, and I know I need to keep moving, or I'm going to fall asleep right here on the couch. Groaning, I climb to my feet and make my way upstairs to shower.

In our bathroom, I stop short when I see one small box sitting on the floor. "Damn," I mutter. "So much for being done." With a heavy sigh, I settle on the floor, pull open the cabinet under the sink, and begin to unpack. It's not until I reach a box of tampons that I freeze.

My hands start to shake when I realize that I've not needed these in well… I don't know how long. My heart starts to race as hope builds in my chest. We weren't trying, but we weren't not trying either. I place my hands over my still-flat belly, and something inside me just knows.

After shoving everything in the box beneath the cabinet, I climb to my feet. I need a test. I need to know. I can't wait. Rushing downstairs, I grab my purse and pull open the door to enter the garage. Stanley's spot is empty, and I mentally calculate how long it will take him to get back. I should have left him a note, but there's no time.

Ten minutes later, I'm in the pharmacy staring at the pregnancy tests. I don't know which one is better, so I grab one of each. Excessive? Absolutely. Do I care? Not at all. Chances are, I'm going to want confirmation of whatever the result is. Although, in my heart, I'm pretty sure I already know. It's not something that I can explain, but now the idea's taken root, I'm certain we're having a baby.

Pulling into the garage, every light in the house is on, and I know that Stanley is pacing the floor, worried about where I could have gone. I grab my pharmacy bag full of pregnancy tests and my purse and push open the door. He's there, tugging it open and then crushing me in his embrace.

"Where were you? I was worried sick. I came home to find you and your car gone. Is everything okay?" He pulls back, and his eyes rake over me.

"I'm fine. I just realized after you left, I needed something, so I ran out to get it."

"Okay." He nods. "Good. Come on. Let's get you fed."

"I need to do something first." He leads me inside and I hold up the bag of pregnancy tests. He takes it from me and peers inside. When he lifts his head, the biggest smile I've ever seen before in my life greets me.

"We're pregnant?"

I shrug. "I'm not sure. I went upstairs to shower, and there was one small box I forgot about on the bathroom floor. When I started putting it away, I found my tampons. I haven't needed them in a while. I don't remember the last time, so —" I shrug again.

"Let's do this." With the bag in his hand, he picks me up, tosses me over his shoulder, and carries me upstairs. "Oh shit, did I hurt the baby?" he asks, sliding me down his body. "I'm sorry. I shouldn't have carried you that way."

"It's fine, Stanley. If I am pregnant, you didn't harm the baby."

"We're having a baby," he says with awe in his voice.

"We're not sure yet," I caution.

He dumps the bag into the bathroom sink. "Which one?"

I laugh. "I don't know! That's why I bought one of each."

He reaches in and grabs one. "Here. We'll start with this one. I'm going to go grab a couple of bottles of water."

"Why?"

"You bought a sink full of tests, baby. I know you. You're going to want to use them all, or at least a good portion of them, to make sure the results are the same."

"It's like a science experiment," I joke, trying to ease my nerves.

He kisses me hard. "I'll be back." His feet bound down the stairs as I tear open the first box and pee on a stick.

By the time he's back, he's not even breathing heavily as I place the stick on the edge of the sink. I eye the tests in the sink, and he jumps into action, moving them so that I can wash my hands.

"Now what?"

"We wait."

He hands me a bottle of water, and I drink half of it. When I hand it back to him, he places the lid back on and sets the bottle on the counter. He then lifts me so that I'm sitting on the counter as well and steps between my legs. He cups my cheeks as he stares into my eyes.

"If it's negative, we'll keep trying."

"We weren't trying," I remind him.

He nods. "Yeah, but we are now." His hands move to rest over my belly. "I can't stop thinking about it, Lena. You, growing our baby inside you. I—yeah, we're trying."

"We might not have to."

"Either way, this is our future. We're going to start a family." He kisses me, and I get lost in him. In the movement of his tongue stroking against mine, the feel of his hard body pressed between my thighs, and his hands that hold me firmly yet so tenderly, it brings tears to my eyes.

"Can we look?" he asks, breaking the kiss and resting his forehead against mine.

"Yeah, we can look."

Reaching over, he grabs the test, and his expression is neutral. I watch him for a reaction, but from the profile, I don't see any change. That is until his eyes find mine, and they're wet with emotion.

"We're pregnant." He crushes me into his chest, and I hold him just as tightly. I plan to take more of those tests, but I feel in my soul, this is real. This is right.

We're starting our family.

# CHAPTER TEN
## *Stanley*

**I** WAKE WITH a jolt and reach for Lena. Thankfully, she's sleeping peacefully next to me. I've been on edge for the last few weeks. Who am I kidding? I've been on edge since the night we found out she was pregnant. I worry about her and our son every day.

Our son.

He's due to arrive any day now. I'm so damn excited to meet him. The nursery is ready, and the bags are packed and in the car along with the car seat. Trust me on this. I've checked what feels like a few thousand times in the last couple of weeks. I'm anxious, and I want to do everything I can to make my wife's delivery better.

It weighs heavily on me that she's doing all the work. She's been a fucking rock star throughout the pregnancy. I know she's uncomfortable, but she never complains. She simply smiles and tells me he's worth it. However, I see her grimaces and how she's moving slower and constantly rubbing her back.

I once thought that I couldn't love her more. Every single day, she proves me wrong.

She moans in her sleep, pulling me out of my thoughts. Reaching over, I start to rub her lower back. She's been having lots of pain in the last couple of weeks. She moans as I apply light pressure, and the sound goes straight to my cock. I ignore my needs because I know she's uncomfortable right now.

She's also never been sexier to me. She doesn't feel that way, I know, but if she could see herself through my eyes, she would know I've never desired her more. Hence the reason I'm ignoring my cock, which is begging to be inside her.

"Gotta pee," she mumbles, tossing the covers off. I'm out of bed and standing at her side to offer her a hand before her feet hit the floor. "Are you part superhero?" She chuckles.

"That's me, superhero husband to the rescue. Up you go." I help her stand, and with my hand on the small of her back, I guide her to the bathroom.

"I'm too tired to argue with you, but in case you didn't know, I live here, too, and I'm able to find my own way to the bathroom."

I bite down on my cheek to hide my grin. This isn't the first time we've had this conversation since we found out she was pregnant. "I like taking care of you." Sure, I take it to the extreme, but again, she's doing all the heavy lifting, being pregnant. The least I can do is make sure all of her wants and needs are met.

She sighs. "I—" She stops midsentence. "Oh shit," she says breathily.

"Lena?"

Her nails dig into my arm that's pressing against her belly while the other rests at the small of her back. "My water just broke."

Panic starts to set it. It's time. We're having a baby. My palms are sweaty and my heart feels as if it could jump out of my chest. Taking a deep breath, I try to remain calm. At least on the outside.

Sure enough, I look down to see there is indeed a small puddle on the floor beneath her that I didn't notice. "Right. Okay. We've got this." I scoop her up into my arms, and she yelps.

"Stanley Riggins. Put me down."

"No can do, baby momma. We have a little boy to meet."

"I can walk down the stairs," she grumbles. "And I'm—messy."

"You're not telling me anything that's changing my mind here, baby. I've got you. I don't give a fuck that you're messy. Let me be messy with you. I'm not leaving your side, and I'll be damned if I'm going to let you walk."

"You're a lot, Stanley Riggins." She sighs, but it's more of a dreamy sigh than an irritated one. She knows this is who I am, at least where she's concerned.

I grin down at her as we hit the bottom step. "I'm yours, Lena Riggins. Are you ready to meet our son?" My heart pounds in my chest. My nerves are on high alert, but I do everything I can to keep them at bay. I'm not worried about being a dad. I know that I can do anything with Lena by my side. I'm worried about my wife. I know labor isn't exactly easy, and if I could, I would step into her place. It's going to kill me to watch her go through this.

"I'm so ready. I'm also scared as hell. We're about to have a tiny person who's going to rely on us for everything."

"You're going to be an amazing mother, Lena. Don't doubt that. Your heart is big, baby, and you have so much of it to give. This little man, he's going to be smothered in love."

She sniffs and wipes at her eyes as I fiddle with the garage door to push it open without letting her go. "Way to make me cry." She smacks at my chest lightly. "Brat."

"Love you." I smile at her.

"I love you too." She returns my smile.

*We're having a baby!*

Carefully, I place her on her feet and pull open the passenger door, helping her inside.

"I should sit on a trash bag or something." She scrunches up her nose while staring down at her lap.

"What?"

"I don't want to ruin the seats."

I kneel so that we're eye to eye. "Listen to me. This car can be cleaned. It's a material possession. I don't want you to worry about anything but bringing our little guy into this world. Let me handle the rest."

"But I'm a mess."

"You're a beautiful mess, wife." I kiss her softly before reaching in and strapping her seat belt. I make one more mental check that I have everything before closing the door on the house and opening the garage door. Whatever I might have forgotten, we can send someone to get it for us. Right now, we need to get to the hospital.

I'm floating. At least that's what it feels like. I was happy the day Lena agreed to be my wife. I was thrilled the day we changed her last name and today... *today*, I don't have words to explain how I'm feeling.

Watching Lena deliver our baby boy was an experience I'll never forget. I held my breath until he took his first, and I knew, without a doubt, I'd never be the same. My dad was right. This is a different kind of love — not just for our son but for Lena too.

My wife is sleeping peacefully, as she should be after the work she put in, while I hold our son against my bare chest. The nurses said it was good for him. So, that's what I'm doing. He's so damn tiny. He grunts around, and I know he's getting hungry. Lena made the decision that she wanted to breastfeed. She asked my opinion, and honestly, I didn't have one. It's a lot on her. From the books I've read, I know that it can be painful at times, and that wasn't a choice I felt like I should have a say in.

I told her I would support her no matter what, and she decided that she wanted to try. The little man latched right on like a pro for his first meal, but I have a feeling he's getting hungry again.

"That's a vision I'll never forget," a groggy voice says.

"Look, buddy, Mommy's awake."

"How are my boys?"

"Perfect. We're perfect. How are you feeling?"

"Sore." She pushes herself up, and I scramble to my feet, cautious of our sleeping son, to help her. "My boobs are heavy."

"I think he's ready too." I place him on the bed next to her, wrap him back up like a little burrito, just like the nurse taught me, and hand him to his momma.

"Now that," I say, sitting on the bed next to her, wrapping my arm around them both, "is a vision I'll never forget."

She laughs softly as she runs the tip of her index finger over his cheek. "We need to give this little guy a name."

"Is there one from the list that's standing out to you now that we've met him?"

"Not really. There are so many good ones, and this is a big deal, Stanley. He's going to be stuck with this name the rest of his life."

"I agree." I smile as I press my lips to her temple.

"What about you? Is there a name that's sticking out to you?"

"One."

She peers up at me. "Do I have to offer sexual favors to get you to tell me?" she teases.

"Hey, now, let's not be talking about that. You're out of commission for six to eight weeks."

"My mouth's not." She smirks.

"Lena Riggins!" I pretend to scold her, and she laughs, making our baby boy jerk in her arms.

"Mommy's sorry. You'll learn we have to tease Daddy to keep him on his toes," she tells our son. "All right, husband, hit me with it."

"Royce. Royce Riggins."

"Royce," she whispers.

"It's a strong name. Has a nice ring to it."

"I love it. I love it so much. Welcome to the world, Royce Riggins."

I snuggle them both in close, pressing a kiss to my wife's cheek as she rests against me while feeding our son. Today has been more than I ever anticipated it could have been. I never knew my heart was capable of this much love.

With each day that passes, I find even more layers to the love this woman has brought to my life. Layer by layer, that love grows stronger.

# CHAPTER

*Lena*

## ELEVEN

S TANLEY HAS BEEN working crazy hours for the last couple of weeks. He's been making sure he's home for dinner and to help put Royce to bed, but he's right back at it after that. So I've officially declared Sundays as family days, and he tries his hardest not to work at all.

The business has grown into more than we ever could have imagined. I'm so proud of him. That's why I took a half day of vacation and picked Royce up from day care early. We're going to stop by and take him lunch. I know he's busy, but I also know that this will be a welcome surprise. Not just for Stanley, but for all of us. We miss him.

"All right, baby boy, are you ready to go see Daddy?" I ask Royce as I lift him out of his car seat.

"Da Da," he yammers.

"That's right." I kiss the top of his head, settling him in the stroller. I make sure to grab my purse, the diaper bag, and the bag filled with our lunch and lock up the car.

"Lena! Hi," Kathy, our receptionist, greets me. "It's so good to see you. And you." She walks around her desk and kneels down to talk to Royce. "You're getting so big." She wiggles his foot, and he giggles.

"I know that sound."

I smile at my husband as he stalks toward us. "Hi, husband."

His eyes heat, which is exactly what I expected with that greeting.

He wraps his arms around me and hugs me tightly before dropping a kiss on my lips. He bends over to kiss Royce on the top of his head. "Not that I'm not happy to see my family, but what are you two doing here?"

"I took some time off. Royce and I decided today was the perfect day to come and have lunch with Daddy."

"This is a wonderful surprise."

"Do you have time to eat with us?"

"I'll make time. Kathy, hold all of my calls."

"You got it, Mr. Riggins."

Stanley slides an arm around my waist and pushes the stroller with the other, leading us down the hall to his office. His desk is covered with pounds of paperwork, and there are three coffee cups on his desk.

"Looks like I came just in time," I tease.

"Yeah." He releases a heavy sigh. "It's more than I ever thought it would be, Lena. I knew I would bust my ass to make this profitable for us, but this—it's so much more. We need to add to the fleet. We're booked and turning down clients. It's… crazy, right?" He laughs, running his hands through his hair.

"So, what are you going to do about it?"

"What do you mean?"

"It's time to level up, right? What can I do to help?"

"I love you, wife. I couldn't do this without you."

"Flattery will get you everywhere," I joke. "But seriously, what do you need?"

"I talked to a business attorney earlier today. I think I'm going to rebrand and go bigger. We have the capital to do both. Now is the time to expand with us having to turn away work, and our waiting list is growing by the day."

"Okay, so what does that entail?"

"Well, I'm thinking of a new name. Something more than Riggins Trucking. That was small time, and this is going to be huge, baby. I can feel it. We got into the business at the right time."

"I won't disagree with that, but it's also you. You're good to the staff, and you work tirelessly to make this place what it is. Your grit and determination are what's making this business a success."

His eyes soften. "Help me think of a new name."

After digging into the bag with his lunch, I pass his over to him before handing Royce a french fry. I take a bite of my own burger, tearing off a small bite for Royce, while I think about options.

"We're thinking big, right? How big? Tell me what you're thinking."

"I want to eventually expand. I want hubs all over the US, maybe even go global at some point."

"Right, so an enterprise of sorts."

He stops eating, his burger halfway to his mouth. "That's it."

"What? What did I say?" I ask, taking another bite of my burger. I'm starving.

"Riggins Enterprises. That's the new name."

I swallow and wipe my mouth. "Riggins Enterprises," I repeat, trying the words on my tongue. "It's got a nice ring to it."

"You're a genius, wife."

"Oh, go on," I say, making him laugh.

"It's perfect. I'll email the graphic designer I use and have him work up a new logo. Hell, I think I'm just going to offer him a full-time job. I know he's been working in marketing for a while now. I could use someone like that on the team."

"I'm proud of you." I finish off my burger, giving the last little bite to Royce with another fry. Tossing my wrapper into the bag, I bend over and dig around in the diaper bag for the small box I shoved in there before leaving the house. Once I have it, I place it on the desk between us.

"What's this?"

"A gift."

"Baby, you're my gift. You and our son. This was exactly what I needed."

"I know, but I think you'll like what I got you too."

"Whatever it is, I'll love it. I love you."

"I love you too, Stanley Riggins. Now open the box." I keep my hands fisted in my lap, but my eyes are on him as he grabs the box. He shakes it, as I knew he would, which is why I stuffed it with tissue paper.

"What is it, Royce? What did Mommy get me?" he asks our son.

"Da Da," Royce says happily as he munches on his fry.

"Daddy loves you, little man."

Tears well in my eyes, but I quickly blink them away. I watch as Stanley opens the lid on the small box and digs around in the tissue paper. When he finds it, his eyes pop up to mine. I nod, feeling the tears threaten to fall.

"We're pregnant?"

I nod again. I can't seem to find my words. Part of that is the excitement of expanding our family. The other part is the wonder I see on my husband's face as he learns he's going to be a daddy for a second time.

Stanley stares down at the pregnancy test in his hands before standing and rounding the desk. He walks to where I'm sitting and kneels. He slides his hand behind my neck while the other wraps around my waist. He doesn't say a word as he rests his forehead against mine.

"Mom, Mom," Royce says. I know it's only a matter of time until he lets his displeasure of being left out of this embrace be known.

Stanley lifts his head and presses a soft kiss to my lips. He then does the same thing to my belly over my clothes. "I'm your daddy, and I love you so much."

"Da Da." This time, I can hear the cry in his voice. He's getting mad. Stanley must hear it too. He jumps to his feet and lifts Royce from the stroller. He rains kisses all over his face.

"You're going to be a big brother, Royce. A big brother," Stanley says, tossing our son in the air and catching him. Royce giggles. His earlier anger at being left out is completely gone. "Give Mommy a kiss." He suspends Royce in the air near my cheek, and he gives me a sloppy kiss.

"Oh, you give such good kisses."

"Thank you, Lena. Just… thank you. For this life, for loving me, for being my biggest supporter, for giving me a partner. I love you more than words can describe."

"I love you too, baby daddy." I stand and hug my boys. "I guess it's a good thing that the business is doing so well since we're going to need more diapers."

Stanley tosses his head back in laughter. I was stressed about how to tell him. I took the test this morning and couldn't hold the information from him for long. I'm glad I did it today, like this. It's the perfect moment. Another we will both always remember.

Standing from my desk, I grab my water bottle for a refill after yet another bathroom break. I'm due any day now, and this little man is sleeping right on his mommy's bladder.

We're having a boy.

Royce just turned two, and I still have everything that was his, and we moved him to a big boy room. It's saved us a lot of money, that's for sure. I read somewhere when I was pregnant with Royce not to give away any baby items until you were certain you were done having kids. I listened and packed away everything he outgrew into totes in the basement. Sure, some of the seasons for clothes might not line up, but that's okay. We have a baby boy nursery ready to go, and Royce got his new big boy race car bed. I wasn't sure if he would sleep there, but to my surprise, he loves it and sleeps all night long. I still have a gate in front of his bedroom door, just as we did with the nursery. The little bugger took a liking to crawling out of his crib at night. We also have one at the stairs, because I worry he might fall down them. If we ever move out of this house, I want a sprawling ranch. Stairs are too big of a worry for this momma.

I take two steps when I feel the wetness between my thighs. At first, I think I've waited too long to get to the bathroom, but the accompanying pain in my lower back and abdomen tells me this isn't me peeing myself.

"Lena?" My coworker, Sandra, stands and comes to where I'm hunched over. "Are you okay?"

"Oh, I'm fine. My water just broke." I laugh.

"What?" Panic flashes in her eyes. Sandra is in her late forties and never had kids. "Oh shit," she mutters. "What do I do?"

"I need a ride to the hospital."

"I'll call an ambulance."

"No." I reach out and place my hand on her arm to stop her. "I don't need an ambulance. We're five minutes from the hospital. You can drive my car, and I'll call Stanley to have him meet us there. You can bring my car back here, and we'll get it later."

"Okay. Right. I can do this. What do you need?"

"Hand me the phone." She moves the phone from my desk to the edge, and I pick it up to call my husband.

"Riggins Enterprises, this is Kathy."

"Hi, Kathy, it's Lena. Can I talk to Stanley?"

"Sure, Lena. Please hold." I wait a few seconds before I hear his voice.

"Lena?"

"It's time," I tell him.

"Are you okay? Dammit, I knew you should have gone on maternity leave."

"I'm fine. I'm closer to the hospital here than I am if I were at home. Sandra is driving me in my car. I'll meet you there."

"Tell her to drive safely. She has my life in that car."

"We'll be fine. I'll see you soon."

"I love you, Lena Riggins."

"I love you too." I end the call and place the phone down. "Okay, let's do this."

"He's perfect," I say, smiling down at my son.

"You're both perfect." Stanley kisses my temple. He's sitting next to me from where I'm lying in the hospital bed. "What are you thinking for names?"

"We're terrible at this." I laugh. "Most parents have names picked out before the baby gets here."

"Yeah, we have a list. I like that we meet them before giving them their names. It needs to fit, you know?"

"I agree. It's our thing."

"Yeah, and it will be for the next one too."

"How many are we having, Mr. Riggins?" My heart feels too big for my chest as I think about our growing family. This life we're building together, it's more than I ever could have imagined that it would be. I don't know how many kids we'll have, but I know in my heart we're not done yet. Our family doesn't feel complete, but we're getting there.

"We'll keep going until our family feels complete. We both hated being only children."

"I like that plan." I stare down at our sleeping baby as I mentally go through our list of names. "Owen. Owen Riggins." He's quiet and calm, almost serene. Owen is a strong name for my strong little man. He's got dark hair like his daddy, and his older brother.

"Welcome to the family, Owen Riggins." Stanley bends to kiss his forehead before doing the same to mine. "Breath by breath, my love for you grows," he whispers. His gaze lifts to mine. "Piece by piece, you manage to steal more of my heart and soul when I thought you already owned it all."

"Breath by breath and piece by piece," I repeat, my voice cracking. My heart is so full it could burst with love and happiness. Our family is growing. We have two beautiful baby boys, who I'm sure are going to be the best of friends. I can't wait to watch them grow up together.

# CHAPTER *Stanley* TWELVE

**T**HIS IS THE life. Our bellies are full, having just finished dinner. My wife is curled up in my arms on the couch as we watch our sons play on the living room floor. Just as we knew he would be, Royce is a great big brother. Owen tries to mimic everything his big brother does. At three and one, they're a handful, but we wouldn't have it any other way.

"Royce, be careful," Lena warns.

"I's am, Mommy," our oldest son replies sweetly.

"Uh-huh." She chuckles. He's being a little rough with Owen as they play with their trucks on the living room floor. Namely, crashing his into

Owen's foot. Owen doesn't seem to care, but it's better to get a handle on it now before Royce decides he needs to crash harder. He loves his little brother, but he's also ornery.

"How's that project you were working on at the office?" I ask Lena.

"It's going. Just lots of red tape."

She used to love her job, and I think she still does, but I know her heart's here at home with the boys. I've mentioned a few times since Owen was born that I think she should stay home with the boys full time. Riggins Enterprises is soaring. We can afford for her to stay home and raise our boys. That's what she really wants. I just need her to understand it's okay. I want her to be happy, and being with the boys does that.

"You know, if you were to stay home with the boys, that red tape would disappear. Instead, you'd get red crayons," I tease.

She laughs, just as I hoped she would. "You work so hard. I need to contribute to our household too."

*What?* I do a double take. "Wait a minute. Hold up." I sit up and turn sideways so that I can see her face. She does the same so that we're eye to eye. "You contribute to this household every damn day, Lena Riggins. You are the glue that holds us together. That has nothing to do with your day job. It has everything to do with the mother and the wife who keeps her family running like a well-oiled machine while working a full-time job."

"I… would just feel guilty. I wouldn't be using my degree, and you'd have to support us."

"No." I'm shaking my head as I speak because I need her to understand. "No. No. No. Baby, listen to me." I take her hands in mine, bringing them to my lips for a kiss as I collect my thoughts. "This business, it's both of us. I might be the one who goes to the office at Riggins Enterprises every day, but, baby, it wouldn't be this successful without you. You helped me get it off the ground and running. You're there to bounce ideas off, and even if your support is more silent since the boys came along and we've expanded, I know it's there. I can feel it with me every single day.

"Why don't you take over at Riggins, and I'll stay home with the boys?" I offer. I'd do it in a heartbeat, but I know my wife. That's not what she wants.

"What? No. I want to stay home with them."

I smile, and she rolls her eyes. "Was that so hard?"

"I just feel guilty."

"Guilty? For raising our sons? For nurturing them? That's what you've always wanted, Lena. To be a mom, to have a family of your own. We're lucky that we can afford for you to raise our boys.

I'm not pressuring you, but, baby, I know you. I know this is what you want."

"I really do."

"Especially with this one on the way." I reach out and place my hand over her belly.

"What are you talking about?"

"We're pregnant," I tell her.

"Did you fall and hit your head today at the office?" she asks.

I wink at her. "Nope."

"We're not pregnant."

"Want to make a wager?"

"Yep. What are the terms, Riggins?"

"You do what you want without guilt. Stay home with them or don't, but really look inside your heart and do what will make you the happiest."

"I already told you what I want to do."

I shrug. "Then we both win. Three babies, you'll have your hands full. I promise I'll do everything I can to help and be here for all four of you."

"Stop." She laughs.

"Prove me wrong."

"Fine. I will. I'll grab a test tomorrow on my way home from work."

"I have one. Or five." I shrug.

"Really?"

I nod. "I can just tell."

"How?"

"These." I reach over and tweak her nipple lightly.

"Stanley! The boys."

I glance down, and the boys are still playing and ignoring us. "You asked," I tell my wife.

"You can tell from my boobs?" she whispers.

"Baby, I know your body better than I know my own. So, yeah, I noticed. I knew you hadn't. You're so busy at work and taking care of us that you've missed the signs."

"Another baby?" Her eyes well with tears.

"The tests are in the bathroom under the sink."

"That's why you rushed straight upstairs to shower when you got home from work?"

"That, and tonight, you get to relax. Go take that test while I give the boys their baths. Soak in the tub, and I'll be in when the boys are in bed."

"Don't you want the results?"

"I already know, Lena. We're having another baby." I kiss her quickly and stand. "All right, boys, time for a bath." I pick Owen up and offer Royce my hand. I should make them clean up their toys, but it's getting late, and my wife and I need to celebrate baby number three as soon as they're asleep.

"Stanley?"

I stop and turn to look at her. She scrambles to her knees to stare at me over the back of the couch. Tears swim in her eyes. "You've made all my dreams come true. I love you. I love our life. I'm so glad it was you. That day, I'm glad it was you."

I can't help it. I need to kiss her. I walk the boys back to her. "Kiss Mommy goodnight." They do as they're told, and then it's my turn. "You're my magic, Lena Riggins." I kiss her softly. Forcing myself to stop, I take my boys upstairs to get them ready for bed.

"Let me tell you a story," I whisper to my newborn son. Lena is sleeping after fourteen long hours of labor. This time, she was induced. She was ten days past her due date, and the doctors decided this was the best course of action.

My wife is a fucking rock star. "Your mommy worked so hard to bring you here safe and sound," I tell our son. That's right, three boys. He's sleeping and doesn't have a care in the world, which is how it should be.

I lift my son to place a kiss on his cheek. Damn, three boys. I know I'm smiling, and I can't help it. Married six years, three sons, a thriving business, and a beautiful home. A home we've quickly outgrown. We moved Owen into Royce's room to leave the nursery open for the new baby. Lena and

I have been talking about moving to another house, a bigger one.

As our business grows and the media gets wind of a husband-and-wife duo who built an empire with one small box truck, well, it tends to bring the vultures out. We'd like a place with more land for the boys to run and play. That's our next adventure as soon as Lena is feeling up to it.

"I love watching you with our boys."

I glance up to see a sleepy, exhausted smile on my wife's face. "Three boys."

Her smile widens. "Three handsome boys just like their daddy."

"We'll keep trying for a girl," I promise her.

"We can keep trying, but I don't care if we have girls or boys. Happy, healthy babies. That's all I want."

"We have three. Does our family feel complete to you?" I ask her.

"I think we have at least one more in us." She laughs.

Warmth fills my chest. "You're not going to hear me complain." I love making babies with her. I love seeing the result of our love grow and thrive in our boys.

"Is there a name from our list you like more than others?" she asks.

"Yeah, actually, I like Grant. Grant Riggins." I stand and walk toward the bed, lowering our son into her arms.

"Grant Riggins. Royce, Owen, and Grant Riggins. Yeah, I like it."

"Me too. It's a strong name to match his older brothers'."

"Speaking of, we need to introduce them." She offers me an exhausted smile.

"Your mom has Owen, and my parents have Royce. They're here with them. Let me go get the boys first so they can meet their little brother."

"We'll be here," she says, smiling down at Grant.

I rush out to the waiting room, say hello to our parents, thank them for keeping the boys, and tell them I'll be back to get them soon. With Owen on my hip at two and Royce, who's four, holding my hand, we make our way back to the room.

"Are you ready to meet your little brother?" I ask the boys.

"I'll teach him all the things, Daddy," Royce tells me.

"I teach too," Owen adds.

"I know you will. Now, remember, he's tiny, and Mommy is real tired, so we need to be easy with both of them, okay?"

"Okay, Daddy," they both reply.

Slowly, I push open the door.

"There's my boys." Lena smiles and pats the bed next to her. Royce looks up to me for permission.

"Easy," I remind him. He nods and rushes to climb on the bed. I move to the other side and place Owen there while I watch over the four pieces of my heart in the hospital bed.

I lean over, kissing Owen's head, then Royce and Grant. Lena smiles and turns her cheek to me as she giggles. I kiss her the same as I did my sons. Kiss by kiss, I show them they are the best parts of me.

We're now a family of five.

# CHAPTER

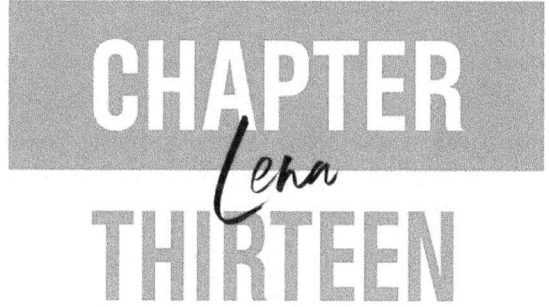

*Lena*

# THIRTEEN

"**L**ENA!" STANLEY CALLS. The front door slams behind him. I can tell from the sound of his voice that it's excitement, not fear. I'm just glad the boys aren't napping because, between his loud voice and the slamming of the door, they would have definitely been woken up by the noise.

"Yes, dear?" I ask sweetly as he steps into the kitchen where I'm icing cupcakes.

He stalks around the island and wraps his arms around me, kissing me soundly. "Hi."

Laughter bubbles up in my chest. "Hi."

"Guess what?"

"We won the lottery?"

"No, but close."

"Really?" I eye him skeptically.

"I found it."

"Found what? Are you feeling okay?" I tease, bumping my hip into his.

"I'm about to make you feel more than okay." He leans down to my level and nips at my ear, causing shivers to race down my spine. All these years later and this man still makes me feel as though I'm a teenage girl getting my first kiss.

"The boys are playing in the living room," I warn.

"I love them, but they're cock blocks," he grumbles.

"Stop." I laugh. "So, what did we win?"

"Well, it's more like luck."

"And that luck would be?" I wipe my index finger over the spatula for the rest of the icing and bring it to his lips. He opens and sucks my finger into his mouth. His eyes are heated, and my panties are ruined. I have no one to blame but myself.

"Well, you know how we've been talking about a bigger house?"

"I do."

"And getting out in the country where the boys can run and play freely with lots of land?"

"We did talk about that," I agree.

"I found it. It's perfect. It's more land than we could ever need to grow and expand, and I can see the boys growing up there, playing outside, just being kids playing in the dirt."

"It sounds like it's everything we've been looking for."

"It is. I was thinking we could pack up the boys and do a drive-by. Maybe we can take them for pizza or something after."

"I'm in. Just let me clean up here and put these cupcakes away."

"I'll go get the boys ready and make sure they're all packed up."

"Thanks, babe." I lean up on my tiptoes, kiss the corner of his mouth, and step away before he can push things further. That will have to wait until we're back home and the boys are in bed.

"Wow." We're standing at the edge of the small gravel path. It's not big enough to be considered a driveway, but the land is gorgeous. It's vast, over one hundred acres. My mind is already racing with the house plans, and Stanley was right: I can see our boys here running and playing and getting into mischief as brothers and little boys do.

It's perfect.

"It's an oasis," Stanley says, rubbing Grant's back. He fell asleep on the way here. All three boys did. They can't resist a car ride. Grant was fussy, even though we left the windows down. He wasn't fully awake, so when Stanley gathered him from his car seat and rubbed his back, he fell right back to sleep.

I should probably wake them up. Our nighttime schedule is in jeopardy, but that's okay. Everything doesn't have to be perfect all the time. Besides, it's nice that Stanley and I can talk about the land without having to look after the boys, making sure they're not getting into anything they're not supposed to. This isn't our property, after all. Not yet, anyway.

"It's so beautiful and peaceful."

"Can you see us living here? Raising our boys here?"

"Yes." There is no hesitation.

"I'm over people walking past the house and stopping me when I'm in the front yard with the boys, asking me to invest in their small business. I get it, but when I'm with my family, that's my time. I don't live for the business, you know?"

"I know. This place is definitely more secluded."

"When I'm home, we could have family time. True family time. I could build the boys a treehouse and… so many things, Lena. Baby, I think we should buy it."

"Okay."

He turns to look at me, his hand resting on Grant's back. He's sleeping soundly in his daddy's arms. I'll never tire of seeing this man be a father to our boys. "That easy, huh? I kind of expected questions and what-ifs."

"I agree with you. With all of it. Our house is too small as it is. Royce and Owen are going to want their own rooms, eventually. I'm over hauling laundry up and down the stairs. I want a one-story."

"Done. Make a list of what you want, baby. I'm about to make all of your dreams come true."

"Oh, Stanley. You already have. You love me with every part of you, and you're the best father to our boys I could ever ask for. We don't need all of this to be happy."

"We don't, but we can afford it, and I want it. I want this little slice of land. I want it to be our safe place to land and be with our boys."

"Call the realtor." There's a buzz of excitement coursing through my veins. I can see it all playing out like a movie reel in my mind. This is where we'll raise our boys. One day, we'll get to sit on the porch and watch our grandchildren running and playing in the yard just as their dads did. This is it. This is where we belong.

"I'm all over it, wife." He kisses Grant's little head and then reaches his free hand out to me. I go to him, settling close to them, while his arm wraps around my waist.

We stand still, just looking at the view. This is about to be our home. This is where we will raise our boys until they're old enough to go out and start lives and families of their own. I can feel it deep in my soul.

This is it. This is where we're supposed to be.

"It's a good thing you insisted on seven bedrooms," I tell my husband as he holds our newborn son in his arms. When he told me he thought we should have seven bedrooms in our new house, I protested, but he eventually convinced me. Now that we have five of them full, I can see the merit.

"Four boys," he says reverently. When he looks up at me, he's grinning. Not that I expected anything less. Stanley is an amazing father, and he loves our sons with everything he has inside him. He loves being their father.

"Four boys." I nod, watching the newest addition to our family get some skin-to-skin time with his daddy. "You're a pro at that by now," I tease. What I don't tell him is that seeing him like that turns me on, and considering I just pushed a watermelon out of my vagina a few hours ago, that's saying something. Then again, it's the Stanley effect. That's what I call it. His hold on me is absolute.

"So are you. You were amazing."

"We make a good team, Mr. Riggins."

His praise makes my heart swell in my chest, but I couldn't do this without him. He truly is my partner in every aspect of our life. He's my rock.

"We are the team, Lena. The fucking dream team." He smirks.

"Language," I scold.

"He's like, two hours old." He chuckles.

"I can see it now. All four of our boys are going to grow up with potty mouths."

He shrugs. "They could do worse."

"You're right. Happy and healthy with potty mouths. I'll take it."

"Well, Momma, what are you thinking for a name for this little guy?" he asks.

"I have so many," I tell him, mentally going through my list of names. "Did you have a favorite?" There are so many it's hard to choose. You'd think after naming three, it would be easier, but here we are.

"There is one that stood out to me." Stanley doesn't take his eyes off our new baby boy.

"Is it a secret?" I tease. He pulls his gaze away and sticks his tongue out at me. "Give me six weeks," I toss out.

"Lena," he growls, and my grin grows.

"Come on, Daddy, let's hear it. What name are you thinking?"

His eyes go back to our son. They're soft and dreamy. It's the look he saves for me and our boys, and it melts my heart every damn time I see it on his face.

"Conrad."

"Oh! That wasn't on my list, but I love it." I repeat it over in my head, and I know instantly that it fits.

"Yeah?"

"Conrad Riggins. It's perfect." He starts to fuss in his daddy's arms. "It's about time for him to eat."

"Yeah. Let me wrap him up. This I am definitely a pro at," he says with a chuckle. "You can feed, and then I'll bring the boys in to meet their new little brother." He stands and wraps Conrad back up in his blanket and places him in my arms. It takes Conrad a few minutes to latch on, but he finally does.

"I love you, Conrad Riggins," I say softly. He stops eating and starts to fuss a little. I hold him closer, trying to soothe him, but his little face is still scrunched up like he's ready to let loose a wail any minute. I pat his bottom, but that doesn't seem to be helping either.

"Hey, buddy, what's going on?" Stanley, who is sitting on the bed next to me with his arm around my shoulders, reaches out and wraps the other around our son so that we're both enfolded in the safety of his arms.

Instantly, Conrad quiets, and he latches back on.

"He just needed his daddy's touch," I whisper.

"Touch by touch, I'll be there for all of you." Stanley kisses my temple, and tears well in my eyes. How is it possible to be this happy? To have this much good in your life? I give all the credit to the man beside me.

Call it magic. Call it luck. I don't care what you call it, because whatever it is, it's also love. So much love, my heart can hardly contain it.

# CHAPTER *Stanley* FOURTEEN

**W**E'VE BEEN MARRIED for nine years today. My mother-in-law took Conrad, and my parents took Royce, Owen, and Grant. At first, Lena didn't want to let them go. She wanted to celebrate our nine years of marriage with the evidence of that love—our sons—but I convinced her that a few hours of "just us" time was what we needed.

With four boys aged seven and under running around the house, it's hard to find adult time, but we make it work. Obviously, we've got our four boys as proof that it can be done. Trust me, we've gotten creative.

"How long has it been since we've sat to eat breakfast together, just the two of us?" I ask, taking a sip of my coffee.

"Royce is seven, so…" Her voice trails off as we both chuckle.

"It feels like yesterday when we first brought him home from the hospital," I reminisce.

"They're growing up so fast." She clears her throat. My wife gets choked up whenever she thinks about how quickly our boys are growing up. When they tell you not to blink because it goes by in the blink of an eye, it's the truth. I can't believe we have a seven-year-old.

"I'm stuffed." Lena pushes her plate to the side. I made biscuits and gravy — one of her favorites — after our parents picked up the boys bright and early. They'd planned to go out for breakfast, all of them before they split ways. "It was delicious, as always. Thanks for cooking." She stands to clear her plate, but I stop her by gently placing my hand on her arm.

"I'm not full yet."

"Oh, okay, I'll make you another plate." She shifts slightly to go back to the kitchen, but my gentle yet firm hold keeps her from moving.

"Nah, only you've got what will fill me up." I tug gently, and she falls into me. Before she knows what's happening, I push my plate away and lift her to sit on the table in front of me.

"Stanley. We eat here." She's laughing and trying to scold me at the same time. It doesn't matter. I don't care.

"That's what I'm doing." I push open her robe, and my wife automatically spreads her legs for me. There's no use in fighting it. I want her, and we're kid-free; time is of the essence. Besides, I can see the need in her eyes. I can hear it in her voice. She wants this just as badly as I do.

I settle her legs on either side of me where I'm still sitting on the kitchen chair and gently run my hands up her calves. "Do you know how hard it was to sit here and watch you eat, moaning around every bite?"

"It was good." She licks her lips.

"You're better." I nip at her thigh, making her laugh.

"There is nothing better than comfort food," she counters.

"I couldn't agree more." Leaning in, I place a kiss on her lower abdomen, just above where we both want my mouth to be.

"So fucking sweet," I murmur. "Lie back, baby." Reaching around her, I push the plates out of the way. I hear them clacking together and the sound of a fork hitting the floor. I'm not sure, but I'm too turned on to care. I'll clean it up later. After I'm full. I smirk at my own thoughts.

"What's that look?" she asks.

"I was thinking about cleaning up what just fell off the table, but I would do it after I've finished my breakfast."

She laughs softly. "You have a big appetite." She bites down on her bottom lip, and my cock thickens.

My hands roam over her body. When I reach her spectacular tits, thanks to our boys, I tweak her nipples, one, then the other, causing her back to arch off the table. I let my fingers trail over her belly, and goose bumps break out across her skin. "I love that after all this time, nine years of being married, I still have this effect on you."

She opens her mouth to say something, what I'm not sure, because I lower my head to taste her. The sweet taste of her pussy explodes on my tongue.

"Stanley," she moans my name. I'm not wasting any time as my tongue presses against her clit. Her legs tighten around my head, and I groan, letting her know how much I love it. I don't let up as I slide one long index finger inside her.

"I want you." She's breathless, and the sound has me increasing my efforts.

I need her to come, because I know that as soon as I'm buried balls deep inside her, I'm not going to last long. Her legs squeeze tighter, which only makes me pump my hand faster.

"S—Stanley, please."

Damn, but I love it when she's needy and begging for me. I suck down on her clit, and that's all it takes. I feel her body convulsing around my hand as her release washes over her. As soon as her legs start to relax, I stand, pull my cock out of my boxer briefs, and push inside her.

I help her to wrap her legs around my waist as I rock gently. She tries to sit up, so I help her. "You feel good wrapped around my cock," I whisper against her lips.

"So good." She nods. I pump into her a few more times, rocking slowly, before placing her back on the table. Her ass is hanging off the edge, giving me room to grip the backs of her thighs as I race toward my release.

I can feel her tightening around my cock, and I grin. She's close. There's nothing better than my wife coming on my cock as I find my release inside her. Moving my hand between us, I gently trace over her clit with my thumb.

"I need you with me, Lena."

She moans, and her pussy squeezes me.

"You gonna come with me, baby?"

She nods, but no words escape her lips. I thrust once more and lose control when she screams out my name. I lose myself inside her as her body spasms around me. At this moment, I truly feel like I'm a part of her, and she's a part of me. So much so, I don't know where she ends and I begin.

Leaning over, I press my lips to hers. I take my time exploring her mouth before finally pulling back and helping her sit up.

"We're really good at that," she says, offering me a lazy smile.

"I agree. We should enlist the grandparents more often."

She nods and bites down on her bottom lip. I can tell there's something she wants to say, but she's hesitant.

"What's on your mind, baby?"

She releases her lip, and a grin lights up her face. "We're going to need a bigger table."

"What?" I laugh. "We can clean this one. No one will ever know."

She nods. "Yeah, but it's not going to be big enough."

"Babe, this table seats eight."

"Yeah, but with five kids and five daughters-in-law, and then you and me, we need at least twelve, and three more if you add in our parents and guests."

It takes me a minute to catch on to what she just said. "Five kids?"

She nods, tears swimming in her eyes as she takes my hand and places it over her belly. "Baby number five."

"When did you find out?"

"This morning. I've been feeling tired, and I'm a few days late."

"Another baby." There is awe in my voice.

This is magic.

Our magic.

"I'll buy you a bigger table." I nod. "You tell me how big you want it, and it's done."

"At least enough for sixteen. My mom might one day find herself a companion." Her eyes mist over. I know she misses her dad every single day.

"Done." I scoop her up in my arms and start for the bedroom. We have a few more hours before we go to pick up the boys. We need a shower, and then, if I'm lucky, I'll make love to her again before we have to clean up the kitchen and the table that's about to be donated because my wife wants one that will seat sixteen.

"Okay, boys, remember we have to be easy with Mommy and your baby brother." I have all four boys standing outside of Lena's hospital room.

"What's his name?" six-year-old Owen asks.

"I'm going to let Mommy tell you what we decided to name him."

"I get to hold him first. I'm the oldest," Royce says.

"I'm next!" Owen says, his six-year-old voice carrying down the hallway.

"Shh, remember inside voices."

"I'm next," he whispers, and I bite down on my cheek to hide my grin.

"Me too, Daddy," Grant says. He's four and mimics every move of his two older brothers.

"Baby," Conrad says, resting his head on my shoulder. He's two and, like Grant, tries his damndest to keep up with his older brothers.

"Everyone will get a chance to hold him." I nod at Royce, and he pushes open the door. I watch as our three oldest boys walk slowly to one side of their mom's hospital bed. Their eyes are wide and full of wonder as they take in their new baby brother.

"He's real little," Royce says.

"You were all this little once," Lena tells him.

"But not me. I'm the oldest." Royce seems to stand a little taller.

Lena laughs softly. "You were still a tiny baby."

"See." Owen sticks his tongue out at Royce. "You were a baby too."

"We've got the pictures to prove it," I say, settling on the bed next to Lena, letting Conrad move to settle at her feet. He's just staring at his momma and the new baby.

"Boys," Lena says, gaining our attention. "Meet your baby brother. This is Marshall."

"I'm glad he was a boy," Owen says.

"Yeah, girls have cooties," Grant agrees.

"What do you know about cooties?" I ask him.

He shrugs. "That's what Royce says."

Lena and I laugh. Right now, they think girls have cooties. Give it a few years, and that will surely change. Royce settles in the chair at Lena's instruction. I lift Marshall from her arms, kiss his tiny nose, and carefully place him in Royce's arms, helping him support his head. Each of the boys takes their turn. They wait patiently, and when they hold him, they tell him they love him.

Not gonna lie, that has me choked up. My heart rate kicks up. My heart is so full of love for our family. Royce and Owen are sitting on one side of the bed, talking to their momma, while Conrad is curled up at her feet. His eyes are heavy, and I know he's about to crash. At two years old, he's the only one of the four who still takes naps.

"Daddy?" Grant asks. He's been on my lap, his head against my chest, just taking it all in. If I didn't know better, I'd think he was ready for a nap as well, but a few months ago, he stopped taking them.

"What's up, buddy?" I push his hair back out of his eyes. It's almost time for a cut. I make a mental note to take all four of the boys once I get Lena and Marshall home and settled from the hospital.

"Why does your heart sound like that?"

"Like what?"

He turns to look at me. "It's doing this." He taps his hand against his chest in a fast rhythm.

I smile at him. "My heart is racing."

He tilts his head to the side. "Why?"

"Because I'm happy. I love you, your brothers, and your mother with my whole heart and sometimes that makes it beat a little faster."

"It's beating really fast."

"That's because beat by beat, my heart works for all of you."

Grant wrinkles his nose. "Daddy, you're silly. Your heart can't work for me." He turns back around as if he doesn't have the patience to deal with me. My gaze goes to my wife, and she's watching with tears in her eyes. She has Marshall resting against her shoulder as she pats his back.

"Beat by beat," she whispers.

I blow her a kiss, making her grin. "What do you think, baby? Is our family complete?"

She looks down at the sleeping baby in her arms. "Yeah, I think it is."

I nod. We've talked a lot since finding out Marshall was a boy. It's not that we kept trying for girls. We just kept making babies because it's the miracle of life and evidence of the love we share. However, we're not getting any younger, and five boys are sure to be a handful in their teenage years. We decided that this would be our last baby, but we both held the right to veto that after Marshall was born.

"The Riggins brothers."

"Our perfect family," Lena replies.

# CHAPTER
## *Lena*
# FIFTEEN

I'M SITTING OUTSIDE on the back porch listening to the crickets. I love this little piece of heaven we've made here. The boys love it too. They spent the entire day outside, running and playing, and it fills my heart with so much joy. I put them all to bed about twenty minutes ago, but Conrad insisted he needed another drink of water just as we were heading out here to have a glass of wine and decompress from the day.

Stanley chuckled at our four-year-old and led him back to his room with the promise of a sip of water. My husband is great with our boys. He is patient and loving, and seeing him with them makes my heart swell.

The patio door opens, and Stanley steps outside. He has the bottle of wine in his hands, and wordlessly, I lift my cup for a refill. "Con asleep?" I ask him.

"Finally. Grant also decided he needed a drink, and Royce heard us and proceeded to tell me from his bed, yelling out the door, that he's ten and shouldn't have to go to bed at the same time as the babies, which means Owen piped up from his room, and said the same." He laughs.

"I swear those kids have super human hearing unless I'm telling them to pick up their toys, or clothes." I'm smiling because it's true, and because I wouldn't change them. Not a single thing. I love every minute of being their mother, and I love even more so watching them grow into their own personalities.

Royce is steadfast and serious. As the oldest, he takes his job very seriously. He guides his younger brothers, teaching them things from sports, to helping them with homework. He also has a tender outgoing side that he reserves for those closest to him. Royce is a born leader, not just because he's the oldest.

Owen is eight, and he's quiet, unless he's around his brothers. He's still the quietest of the five, but those eyes of his tell me he's taking it all in, watching and learning every single day. He's a wiz at numbers, and his teachers keep telling me how advanced he is and that we should bump him up a few grades. Stanley and I discussed it, and we don't want that. We want him to be exactly who he is. An eight-year-old little boy who loves math. We want him to be eight, not eighteen. I know that they're all going to grow up, but I want that to be as slowly as possible.

Grant, who is six, is a mix of all five of my boys. He's the one who can be serious like Royce, or silly like his younger brothers. He's the middle brother, and he's like a sponge, soaking up as much time as he can get with the older two, but never refuses to play or help his younger brothers. He has a sweet tooth that is for not only sweets, but for life.

Conrad is four, and he's such a hoot. He's ornery and sweet at the same time. He looks up to his three older brothers and tries to boss his youngest around like it's his job. He's always acting silly to get us all to laugh or gain our attention. He's outgoing and doesn't know a stranger.

Marshall, the baby, is two, and he's the one that completed our family. He loves to snuggle, and I just know his heart is going to be huge, with all the love he has to give. He tries to mimic everything his four older brothers do, and it's rather comical. He's two going on twelve, but I guess that's to be expected with older brothers.

All five of my boys are unique in their own ways, and it thrills me to watch them grow into their own personalities. Being a mother is something I always wanted to do and those five boys, and their daddy, they've given me so much happiness and love in this lifetime.

"What are you thinking about over there?" Stanley asks me.

"Just about life. How fortunate we are."

Stanley reaches over and offers me his hand, and I take it. We're sitting on the double lounger that my husband insisted we needed because us having each our own was me being too far away from him. I acted like I was letting him have his way, when really, inside, my heart was flopping around in my chest. We've been married for twelve years and have five amazing sons, and this man—my husband still causes me to swoon over the things he does and says to me. We're still us from before kids, and I know without a shadow of a doubt we'll still be us when we're sitting here on this back porch in thirty years. It's a bone deep feeling in my gut, and I always trust my gut.

"I love you, Lena Riggins."

I smile up at the night sky. "I love you too."

"Babe, I want to run something past you." Stanley comes walking in the door. He took the boys on an adventure on our land, giving me some time to do some deep cleaning in the house. He actually suggested I take the boys so he could do the deep cleaning he knows I've been wanting to do, but I told him to go. I enjoy cleaning, and he doesn't get to spend as much time with the boys as I do. It's a win-win for all of us.

"What's up?" I ask as I finish folding the final load of laundry. For now, that is. With seven of us in this house, laundry is never-ending.

"I want to dig a pond. A really big pond. Okay, probably more like a lake."

I can't help the laughter that bubbles out of me. "You want to build a lake?"

"Yes." He nods, his face serious.

"Tell me more." I put the towels in the closet in our master bathroom, and move to sit next to him on the bed, giving him my full attention.

"Think about it. We could get a boat, which is why we need a lake. It would be a pontoon, oh maybe bigger, yeah, we'll need a speed boat too so we can all relax, but the boys could water ski. We could buy a couple of jet skis too."

"That all sounds like fun," I tell him.

He nods. "This place is our own little oasis, and adding the lake would give the boys something else to do. Think of all the summer fun."

"What brought this on?"

"We were hiking through the woods, and Grant asked about fishing. That's something else we could do. We could set up tents next to the lake and do some night fishing. It'll be great."

"Okay."

"Okay?"

I smile. "You don't need my permission, Stanley. This is something you want. I say go for it."

"I'll build you a gazebo," he adds. "I know how much you loved the pier from our honeymoon, and we'll do something similar with a gazebo out on the water."

I stand and move to step in front of him. He opens his legs, and his hands grip the backs of my thighs, pulling me close as I run my fingers through his hair. "I love you. Not for the things you give me, but for the way you love me and our boys. I mentioned that years ago, Stanley Riggins."

"I never forget anything where you or our kids are concerned." He tilts his head back and I kiss his lips.

"Well, it looks like we're building a lake."

"It's going to add value to the property, not that we would ever want to leave here, but I can see it, baby. The boys having a blast all summer long. It's going to be so much fun."

My husband is still a big kid at heart. I think I am too, and seeing his eyes light up when he talks about his plans for our lake, I can't help but join him in his excitement. I'm all for anything that keeps my boys here and entertained.

I love the idea of having this be our own place, not having to worry about outsiders or drunk drivers on other boats. I hope that the boys continue to come here and enjoy this space once they're out on their own.

# PRESENT *Stanley* DAY

"**W**HAT ARE YOU smiling about, old man?" Marshall, my youngest son, asks me.

"I'm happy." How could I not be? I have the world's most beautiful, loving wife. We have five amazing sons, and with those sons, we gained five incredible daughters. And the cherry on top of the cake is our grandchildren. We have ten grandsons and nine granddaughters. Nineteen grandchildren. That's a whole hell of a lot to be smiling about.

"What's going on over here? Is this a meeting of the minds or what?" Conrad asks.

"Dad's all smiley and it's creeping me out." Marshall laughs.

"What's creeping you out?" Grant asks, joining the conversation. He hands the three of us a beer, leaving one for himself.

"That." Conrad points at me.

"I see how it is. Y'all have a meeting about manly things and don't include the two older and wiser brothers," Owen says as he and Royce join us.

"What are we talking about? Taking the boat out?" Royce asks. "I know the kids have been begging since we finished lunch."

"No. Look at him." Grant points at me.

Owen and Royce both turn to face me. "Why are you smiling like that?" They ask at the same time. It makes me laugh while their three younger brothers nod their agreement.

"This right here—" I wave my arms to where my wife, our daughters-in-law, and our grandkids are all sitting beneath the pavilion at our lake. "This was my dream. To raise our family here and to one day watch as you boys did the same. I have a hell of a lot to be smiling about."

They're all quiet, but I see each of them nod. We sit quietly, watching as those we love the most run and laugh and play. It's music to my ears.

"You know, when you told me that my first wife, let's not bring her name into this day, wasn't my magic, I thought you were losing your mind. I grew up listening to you talk about it, but I thought you and Grandad were shooting the shit, telling tall tales. Then I met Sawyer." He stops talking as if he needs to collect his thoughts, and we all remain silent, letting him work through them.

"When I met Sawyer, my entire world flipped upside down. She changed me, and she changed my view of the world. That's when I knew the magic of love you'd talked about my entire life was real. I wish I would have listened to you then."

"Ah, words that every parent loves to hear." I chuckle. "Royce, that was your path to Sawyer. I truly believe that. Sure, you fought against it, but you can't outrun the magic."

"Tell me about it." Owen snickers. "Even when they're wearing shoes with holes."

We all laugh. We can laugh about it now, but my daughter-in-law Layla was in a rough way when Owen met her. He felt the connection instantly and fought for her.

"It took me a few days, but less time than it did Royce to realize what was happening." He points his beer at me. "I knew when I couldn't stop going back to the restaurant that something was different and that you and Royce were on to something."

"I didn't fight it," Grant speaks up. "I mean, the magic of my wife's sweets was more than enough to convince me she was meant to be mine."

We all laugh. Grant has always had a sweet tooth, so it's fitting that he found his magic with the owner of a bakery.

"Took me a little longer," Conrad confesses. "I can't believe she was right there under my nose for months, and I never realized she was the one for me."

"You weren't ready for her. Just like Royce wasn't ready for Sawyer. It all has a way of working out," I tell him.

"Yeah, I got the girl. Thank fuck for snowstorms." He laughs.

"I got you all beat," Marshall speaks up. "I got double the magic with Maddie and Wren. She made me work for it. Her heart needed time, I guess." Marshall shrugs.

"It did." I nod. Wren had also been through so much and was struggling to find her place when Marshall came into her life. Little Maddie stole our hearts, and his, just like her momma.

I finish off my beer and toss it into the recycling bin. Leaning forward, I rest my elbows on my knees and make eye contact with each of my five sons.

"I love you. The five of you, your momma, and your families are my greatest gifts in this life. I'm so damn proud of each of you for the men you have become, the husbands and the fathers. That's why I'm smiling."

"Way to get us in our feels, old man," Marshall says, clearing his throat.

"Damn allergies," Grant mumbles, looking out at the lake.

"Come on. Enough of the heavy. Let's get that boat out on the water and have some fun." I stand, and Royce does immediately as well, pulling me into a hug. He releases me, and Owen takes his place. Then Grant, Conrad, and Marshall all take their turns.

"I love you, old man," Royce says, and his brothers repeat their "I love yous," just as they did when they were little.

My heart is full.

Breath by breath, these five men have a piece of me no one else ever will.

*Thank you for taking the time to read*
**Breath by Breath**.
*This story has been a long time coming and I'm so excited I finally found the time to write it. I've had the cover image for years, so it was definitely time.*
*I loved going back to this world.*
*Thank you for loving the Riggins family as much as I do.*

*Never miss a new release.*
*Subscribe to Kaylee's mailing list and be first to hear about free content, new releases, cover reveals, sales, and more:*

www.kayleeryan.com/subscribe/

*More about Kaylee's books:*

www.kayleeryan.com/books/

# CONTACT *Kaylee* RYAN

**Facebook:**
http://bit.ly/2C5DgdF

**Instagram:**
http://bit.ly/2reBkrV

**Reader Group:**
http://bit.ly/2o0yWDx

**Goodreads:**
http://bit.ly/2HodJvx

**BookBub:**
http://bit.ly/2KulVvH

**Website:**
www.kayleeryan.com

**OTHER WORKS** *by* **KAYLEE RYAN**

### With You Series:

Anywhere with You | More with You
Everything with You

### Soul Serenade Series:

Emphatic | Assured | Definite | Insistent

### Southern Heart Series:

Southern Pleasure | Southern Desire
Southern Attraction | Southern Devotion

### Unexpected Arrivals Series

Unexpected Reality | Unexpected Fight |
Unexpected Fall | Unexpected Bond |
Unexpected Odds

### Riggins Brothers Series:

Play by Play | Layer by Layer | Piece by Piece
Kiss by Kiss | Touch by Touch | Beat by Beat
Breath by Breath

# OTHER WORKS *by* KAYLEE RYAN

**Out of Reach Series:**
Beyond the Bases | Beyond the Game
Beyond the Play | Beyond the Team

**Entangled Hearts Duet:**
Agony | Bliss

**Cocky Hero Club:**
Lucky Bastard

**Mason Creek Series:**
Perfect Embrace

**Standalone Titles:**
Tempting Tatum | Unwrapping Tatum | Levitate
Just Say When | I Just Want You | Reminding Avery

Hey, Whiskey | Pull You Through | Remedy
The Difference | Trust the Push | Forever After All
Misconception | Never with Me

# OTHER WORKS by KAYLEE RYAN

*Kincaid Brothers Series:*
Stay Always | Stay Over | Stay Forever | Stay Tonight
Stay Together | Stay Wild | Stay Present
Stay Anyway | Stay Real

*Everlasting Ink Series:*
Does He Know? | Is This Love?

## Co-written with Lacey Black:

*Fair Lakes Series:*
It's Not Over | Just Getting Started
Can't Fight It

*Standalone Titles:*
Boy Trouble | Home to You
Beneath the Fallen Stars | Tell Me A Story

*Co-writing as Rebel Shaw with Lacey Black:*
Royal | Crying Shame | Watch and Learn

# ACKNOWLEDGEMENTS

There are so many people who are involved in the publishing process. I write the words, but I rely on my team of editors, proofreaders, and beta readers to help me make each book the best that it can be.

Those mentioned above are not the only members of my team. I have photographers, models, cover designers, formatters, bloggers, graphic designers, author friends, my PA, and so many more. I could not do this without these people.

And then there are my readers. If you're reading this, thank you. Your support means everything. Thank you for spending your hard-earned money on my words, and taking the time to read them. I appreciate you more than you know.

Special Thanks:

Becky Johnson, Hot Tree Editing.

Julie Deaton, Jo Thompson, and Jess Hodge, Proofreading

Lori Jackson Design – Main cover and special edition design

Furious Fotog – Photographer (Main Guy Cover)

Chasidy Renee – Personal Assistant

Megan Davis – Graphics and assistance

Jamie, Stacy, Lauren, Franci, and Erica

Bloggers, Bookstagrammers, and TikTokers

Lacey Black & Kelly Elliott

Stacy and Ms. Betty - Graphics

The entire Give Me Books Team

My fellow authors

And my amazing Readers

With Love,

*Kaylee Ryan*
AUTHOR